THE MOLE PEOPLE

By Kevin Landt

Part One

"Suzie Schizo"

Chapter 1: The Two Little Girls

"Suzie Schizo! Suzie Schizo!"

The sing-song chant echoed throughout the university lecture hall, the familiar mockery of her name making Suzie cringe in her seat. Two little girls stood at the doorway, their school uniforms ill-fitted and their pigtails askew. Their faces were indistinct, but the cruel delight in their voices was unmistakable.

Suzie sat as calmly in her seat as she could, attempting to ignore them. She glanced at the young man seated next to her. He seemed bored by the professor's lecture, yet completely undisturbed by the intruders.

The girls continued to chant, their voices growing louder, but no one else appeared to notice. Not the professor, with his monotone voice droning on about English Literature, not the students, scribbling notes with feverish intensity.

"Suzanne? Are you listening to anything I'm saying? I've asked you the same question twice!"

Suzie looked up, the noise in her head clearing a bit, though the girls' voices didn't stop. Their blurred figures hovered in the doorway, their white ankle socks grubby, hair escaping their pigtails. One wore a pink dress, the other a sunflower yellow dress, though by now, Suzie knew enough about herself to guess they were just a figment of her troubled mind.

"Suzie Schizo! Suzie Schizo! Where does your mind go?" They would chant in unison; two girls from her sixth grade class whose names she couldn't recall. Their faces were equally blurred in Suzie's memory, though their childish spite still reverberated across the years. They would follow Suzie as she walked home alone. Always alone.

She chewed on a fingernail, her normal method of distracting herself from what her brain was yammering on about, from the ringing in her ears that just would not stop, that never stopped. Normal. It was not usually a word associated with Suzie.

Those girls were right, though they didn't know it at the time. Their diagnosis at the age of twelve or so, when their only intention was to make her suffer, to exclude and punish her for her strangeness, was correct, something Suzie discovered many years later.

Suzie couldn't remember a time when she was not considered odd, different. Kids used to chant "Suzie Schizo"—and worse—throughout middle school; on the playground, on the sports field, in the cafeteria—or the café-fearia as she called it then. Lots of mean things went on in school cafeterias. She wondered if it was something in the water. Or the juice boxes.

She'd always inhabited a different world. For years, she wondered why she was always alone, why she wasn't happy when everyone around her seemed okay and able to 'fit in' and 'be normal'. When she was diagnosed at the age of twenty, only a couple of years ago, suddenly everything made sense:

The voices that no one else heard. The shadowy figures following her, the paranoia, the fears, the confusion, the sights and sounds she was told were not really there, the searing depressions that left her floundering, the strange thoughts, and the loneliness. It was all explained by this official recipe of her brain, as she liked to call it.

The diagnosis was a relief—sort of. In a session with her third psychiatrist, she'd asked dryly, "So I'm not just some freak?"

"No, Suzie, you have schizophrenia," he replied.

"Schizophrenia, huh? … I like that. That's a nicer way to put it, I think."

Schizophrenia: the root of all her evils. Sometimes the diagnosis made sense. But other times:

"Schizophrenia," she shouted at Psychiatrist Number Five, her voice shaking with anger, "that's what my last psych told you to say, isn't it?"

"No, Suzie."

"It's pretty convenient how you all say the same thing. Just say that magic word and Suzie'll feel better, right?"

Sometimes she wondered if she was actually special, tuned in to a higher realm, able to hear wisdom and messages from the angels. Sometimes, she cut herself just to remember she was still alive, to feel something. Sometimes she downed a bottle of wine to stop feeling anything at all.

"Ms. Franks! I ask you again to tell us some of the ways in which Shakespeare is relevant to contemporary society? Is his work relevant? And if not, why not?"

The voice was British, male, and boomed across the stately auditorium. Suzie started out of her thoughts and memories, momentarily dazed by them. Everything in her mind felt so real, but she knew she couldn't trust herself. Her mind lied to her. It told her odd stories. It conspired against her, just like all the others, just like those girls, who called her crazy. At least now, she had a label, a diagnosis, a reason for her strangeness —though she wondered if that was a lie too.

Suzie blinked, her gaze drifting around the room as if searching for something solid to anchor her thoughts. She was never quite sure of anything. She was never quite sure what was real, and what was not, what was truth and what could be just another deception. She was never quite sure if, in fact, she might be the sane one—more normal than anyone else, maybe? Or, perhaps, everyone around her was crazy.

That thought, at least, gave her comfort. Anyway, who could prove she wasn't the sane one?

The lecturer, Professor Rami, was standing at his gilded podium at the front of the lecture hall, staring at her. She could hear students around her snigger, including those two schoolgirls who mocked her from the edge of the hall. Rami was six feet tall and wore a brown sports coat over faded blue jeans. He was trying to look hip. He was trying to look like one of his students rather than the fifty-something balding dinosaur he really was.

"Ms. Franks, did you actually read last week's assignment?" Professor Rami peered over at her. She felt like she was back in high school, and it was definitely not a good sensation.

"Shit," was all she said, almost absent-mindedly. Then a thought arose. "With all due respect, aren't plays meant to be seen, performed on stage? Reading it is like going to a movie theater, and instead of watching on the screen, we whip out copies of the script..."

There was silence in the hall now, except for the buzzing sound that was growing in Suzie's mind. It sounded like all the voices that spoke to her, that commanded and tormented her, had joined together and blurred into one. She looked down at the nail she'd chewed to its ragged end. No nail polish. Nasty chemicals. Not to be ingested by nail biters.

"And how relevant can a guy who wrote with a quill be in our age of smartphones. Not very..." But as Suzie said this, the room started to swim in front of her eyes and the urgent beat of panic took over. She had to get out of there. She couldn't breathe with everyone watching her.

"Thank you, Ms. Franks, for that insightful analysis of the great bard's work. Can anyone tell me how and why Shakespeare is still important more than four-hundred years after his death?" The professor's voice trailed off in Suzie's mind.

She gritted her teeth, and before she could stop herself, she blurted out: "Nobody, like nobody, uses a quill anymore. We have computers and smart phones, tablets, and social media. How could Shakespeare be relevant to this world and all the shit we've created? We're social lemmings now. We have no subtlety or truth. Even my neighbor's seven-year-old niece has followers on TikTok. Now, that's crazy…"

As the words left her mouth, speeding up as her thoughts jumbled together, she realized people were snickering.

"See me after class, Ms. Franks…" the balding dinosaur said, turning to another student. His eyes were cold, gray, condescending.

"Whatever. Just let me get the hell outta here…"

Suzie Franks, mistress of her own words, if not her own head. She stared defiantly at the sea of faces that were now looking up at her. This was bullshit. She didn't sign up for Freshman English in college to sit through this. This was *soooo* high school—and there, they did the same thing. They laughed at her, called her crazy.

She realized now she was standing. Scrambling, she grabbed her backpack and shoved the thick textbook, her laptop (still in its case), and various pens into it. One of the pens fell to the floor and she kicked it away. The whispers started as she moved, shoving through the tangle of legs and designer bags to the end of the seating area.

The professor was frowning, but she saw something else on his face, something akin to pity. They knew why she couldn't concentrate. They knew of her struggles, but they told her there were ways she could manage them—with the right medication.

"I'm not going to take any drugs," Suzie had informed one of the psychs, she couldn't remember which one.

"Why not?"

"Don't trust them. How do I know they won't turn me into some kind of zombie?"

"That's not what—"

"How do I know they won't block out the good thoughts? Sometimes I feel great, inspired, like I could change the world."

"But what usually comes after that, Suzie?" the psych responded, referring to her moments of deep depression.

"Why are you guys always pushing the drugs?" she'd replied pointedly.

You always had to be careful. Deception was everywhere. Consider color-blindness. How could anyone prove they could see what someone else couldn't? It wasn't possible! So, no, she'd decided she wouldn't take their meds. She didn't trust them—not the psychs (no matter how friendly they tried to appear) and not the drugs. She didn't trust anyone—except Robbie that is.

The bright and airy campus of Hudson University was nestled in the city of Portland, Oregon, home to free thinkers and students, to a buzzing metropolis of creatives, independent shops, and self-proclaimed weirdos.

Moving here as a young child, Suzie couldn't remember living anywhere else – and when her mental health condition was diagnosed, it was here that her mother Dana insisted she stay for college.

"No point leaving now," Dana had said, or something like that.

Suzie, who had grown from a skinny, awkward kid into a rangy, slim adult with long dark hair and pale skin, had looked at her, and shrugged. "No point leaving," she might have agreed.

At least, that was how Suzie remembered—or mis-remembered—the conversation. Or perhaps the entire thing had been fabricated by her noxious neurons, the same neurons where the fragments of her memory and pain, of experience and make-believe, jostled and fought in the maelstrom that made up her delicate sanity.

That sanity was now dancing away from her as she pushed past the backpacks and legs, the designer shoes, and grubby combats.

"Ms. Franks! Leave now and you risk failing this class!" the professor's voice boomed as she fled the room. The familiar sting of embarrassment and frustration washed over her. He said more stuff, but Suzie couldn't see his lips move, and so she knew that the psychosis was adding its own sour spin. She felt again the desperate urge to get out, to breathe the fresh air outside and run back to her dorm room.

With her heart racing and palms slick with sweat, Suzie stumbled outside, gasping, almost retching. She collapsed onto an iron bench, the college buildings' intricate architecture seemingly closing in around her, their shadows dancing in the brilliant sunlight. Students milled past, holding books, chatting, sipping paper cups of coffee.

Time slid onward and Suzie began to settle down, to come back to herself again. The autumn sun was warm on her face. The trees were turning flamboyant red, orange, and brown, their leaves curling as the season changed. *None of this matters,* she thought. *None of them matter at all, because I have Robbie.*

Chapter 2: Robbie

"Suzie? What are you doing in there?"

Bang! Bang! Bang!

The door to their shared dorm bathroom shook with the impact of Andrea's fist.

"Come on, I need to use the bathroom," Andrea moaned loudly. Andrea moaned a lot. Everything Suzie did seemed to be a source of irritation to Prom Queen Andrea, the girl voted most popular in high school, and the one with shiny long blonde hair, gleaming white teeth, and a permanent tan that—despite the Portland winters—never seemed to fade.

Suzie still couldn't figure out how they'd become friends. They were an unlikely pairing. Suzie had black hair and pale skin, was whippet thin and wore long-sleeved black clothes to hide the marks from the blades she used to cut herself. She was the polar opposite of blonde Andrea.

Yet, on the first day of college they hit it off, albeit in an awkward way, when they discovered they liked the same obscure bands. Andrea had no idea Suzie had schizophrenia, until after they'd paired up and were sharing their space. It was her frequent trips to the college counselor that finally alerted Andrea to the fact her roommate was battling with more than just the normal angsts of college life, like who liked whom, or which classes they were bound to fail. When Suzie broke the news, Andrea shrugged. They were sitting in the cafeteria scrolling through their smartphones, when Suzie just said it.

"I've got schizophrenia."

Andrea looked up.

"Er, what?" she said, more interested in her Instagram feed than Suzie confiding in her.

Suzie was surprised too. She definitely did not like sharing her secrets, or any part of herself, with anyone.

"Yeah, so it's a mental illness but I kinda manage it…"

This time, Andrea stared back at her roommate—all thoughts of the influencer she was trying to emulate gone from her mind. Without saying anything, she picked up her phone again and googled it.

"Schizophrenia is a mental health condition where you may see, hear or believe things that are not real…" She looked up at Suzie. "Dude, that explains *a lot*," she said, making them both giggle.

"Yeah, it kinda does." Suzie grinned.

"That's a bummer. So, does it mean you're officially crazy?" Andrea took a long lock of her hair and coiled it in her finger as she spoke.

Suzie nodded. "Yeah, I guess so, but you've always known that, right?"

They'd smiled at each other, but there was something growing behind Andrea's smile that time, she could sense it even then. Something that Suzie recognized more and more from people. It was uncertainty, or fear even.

Suzie felt afraid right now. Crouching still in the dank shower stall, knees gripped near her chin, the *drip, drip* of cold water from the shower head that no one seemed willing to fix.

"Suzie, come on! What are you doing in there? You've been in there like an hour already."

Andrea banged on the door again, this time even louder.

Suzie lifted her head up, though it felt heavier than a bowling ball, and heard her friend groan. Then she heard her slump back onto her bed, waiting. Now Suzie sighed, exhaled, then dropped her head onto her knees again. *Just five more minutes.*

"I'm coming, give me a minute…" Suzie called out eventually, but even she didn't believe herself. Even though the space was small, smelled musty, and was dark and cold, she couldn't seem to leave.

Her thoughts had followed her around like paper planes all day, tapping at her head, swarming as she'd sat through her classes. Now, they crowded around her and within her, demanding she pay attention. This was the only place she could allow them free rein: away from prying eyes, alone and 'safe', contained. Suzie heard whispers but assumed they were a creation of her mind. The thoughts and questions spilled out now. The voices had just been talking, but now they were yelling.

Why would Robbie want to be with you? Doesn't he know how crazy you are? Perhaps he's just leading me on, making fun of me? Everyone knows I'm labelled 'undateable'—they tell me often enough—so why is Robbie asking me out and suggesting we go places? There must be a reason? He can't actually like me? I'm broken. I'm weird. I don't fit in anywhere. He must be laughing at me. This must be some kind of joke with his soccer jocks…

Suzie shook her head, as if she could shake the thoughts from her brain. The questions kept tripping over themselves, in their rush to be noticed, but she couldn't think them clearly enough to do anything about them. Her head lied. Her brain did its own thing. The counselors said she should start taking meds as soon as possible, but Suzie was scared. She feared they were lying to her, and if she took something, her brain would only get weirder. Perhaps it was even a trick to control her.

Suzie sighed again. She was getting ready for another date with her boyfriend Robbie, the guy everyone wanted to be with, and the guy who had chosen her, much to everyone's surprise. Even though Suzie was pretty in a slight, troubled kind of way, she was odd and not particularly liked. Andrea was one of her only friends, so she was thinking that Robbie didn't get the memo that she was too weird to go out with.

Suzie smiled then as she thought of Robbie. He was a jock, a man's man—except he wasn't, not really. The side he showed to Suzie was so different from his public image of a sports-loving, beer-guzzling, laugh-out-loud popular guy that it took her breath away to know that underneath all that was a tender, sweet-hearted young man, one who liked to hold Suzie's hand and whispered sweet things to her, especially when she was veering toward feelings of paranoia or panic.

For months, Robbie kept trying to catch Suzie's eye in class or at lunch. Suzie's cheeks flushed with embarrassment, assuming he was teasing or mocking her, and so she never looked back. She always turned away until one day she couldn't avoid him. Nestled beneath a willow tree on the lush college grounds, Suzie savored an apple while debating whether to skip class, just as an imposing shadow loomed over her.

"Hey, you're Suzie, right?"

It was Robbie.

He walked over to her and started speaking in that easy way he does. She blinked up at him, trying desperately to figure out why he was trying to talk to her, the lunatic girl on campus.

He didn't wait for her reply. He settled beside her, dropping his bag carelessly on the verdant grass, his blue eyes twinkling with warmth.

"So, what classes are you in? I've seen you around…" His manner was relaxed. He didn't seem to be making fun of her, though Suzie looked around to check he didn't have a gaggle of teammates watching them or sniggering from the side lines. Nope. No one else seemed to be taking any notice of them.

"Erm, I'm majoring in English," Suzie stuttered.

"Cool. That's cool," Robbie replied. "My major's Business, but I like the lectures so I pop in now and then, see what's going down in English. Shakespeare was a really cool guy. He invented loads of words that we still use today, just so cool, but I guess you know that already." He grinned.

Suzie didn't know what to say. All she kept thinking was: *Why are you bothering with me? Why are you even talking to me like you're not embarrassed to be seen with me?*

Robbie didn't appear to notice her impression of a deer struck dumb, mesmerized in the road by the headlights of the car about to mow it down. As she stared at him, wide-eyed, he kept on chatting, pushing his thick blond hair off his tanned face. Suzie observed his generous, full lips and eyes that mirrored the azure sky above. If he realized she was staring, he was too polite to say.

Robbie had been drawn to Suzie from the first moment he saw her in the cafeteria, not long after they started college. She had been talking to her friend, who was the classic high school beauty, with sun-kissed hair and white teeth—all so *blah blah*. The blonde girl had been chatting away as Suzie, dark and pale, was listening, eyebrows arched, looking like she would be happier anywhere else but here.

None of his friends could understand Robbie's attraction to the 'weird girl' in black, but Zane Martin, captain of Hudson's football team, put it less charitably:

"…your freak crush," he spat.

It was on the sports field, during a regular dispute between soccer and football over which team would use the field for practice that day. Robbie suspected Zane instigated these skirmishes out of a thinly-veiled insecurity; Robbie had led the soccer team to an undefeated season so far, while Zane's leadership had produced just a single win. Nevertheless, all the attention and glory still went to the football team, naturally.

"Yeah, she's different," Robbie replied evenly, standing fully upright to heighten the effect of his imposing frame. "But I like that. She's not predictable—and that makes her interesting—a challenge. You could never handle her."

Robbie thought that underneath the strangeness and the emo get-up, Suzie had more going for her. He wanted to find out, anyway, though he did regret the effect on his social standing.

It had taken him weeks to approach her, as she always seemed in a hurry, going somewhere, brushing off anyone who tried to speak to her. Today, was the first day he had found her somewhere peaceful, somewhere where she couldn't pretend she was too busy or hadn't seen him.

"So, what are you doing on Friday? There's a party that night. It's going to be so lit. All the kinds of music you like…" Suzie often wore band t-shirts tied at the front against her petite waist.

Suzie had looked at him, panicked, but before she could say 'no,' something surprising happened—the words 'yeah, sounds great' came out of her mouth. Before she could change her mind, Robbie, perhaps sensing her unease, jumped up, grabbed his bag and replied: "Awesome. I'll swing by your dorm around eight. See you then…"

"See you," Suzie echoed, wondering what the hell had just happened.

The party—or the date to be precise—had gone well, though Suzie was nervous. So when she was offered a drink, she reached out and took it. She drank more than she was intending to. By the end, the surprise of seeing the two together had abated, as everyone got more drunk, and Robbie walked her back to her dorm. He didn't even attempt to kiss her.

That night, for once, the voices seemed to fade away, though Suzie wasn't sure if it was the alcohol or Robbie, or the combination of both, that had brought about this unexpected relief. Of course, the voices did come back, like the tide pulling back from the shore, by the next day, but something inside Suzie had changed. She felt different. She felt like someone, *someone*, had seen her for who she really was, and hadn't turned away. More than that, it was possible he'd even *liked* her for being this way.

"Looks like you had a good night," Andrea had said the day after, pointedly. She looked grumpy and was still in her pajamas, though it was way past noon. Usually she'd be out shopping with her gaggle of wanna-be Instagram models, taking selfies and drinking coffee.

"Yeah, it was good. You?" Suzie had said, wrapped in her duvet, wondering whether to go back to sleep or get up.

"My date ended up getting so drunk I found him making out with Delaney in the kitchen. Asshole. I'm so sick of these college boys. They always let me down," she said.

"Ah, I'm sorry to hear that," Suzie said.

Later, when Suzie had dragged herself out of bed and wandered to the campus dining hall, she felt a tap on her shoulder.

"Hey, so we had a great time last night. How's the hangover?" Robbie smiled. Suzie felt her heart leap, which was a first.

She hesitated for a moment, then said, "Uh, yeah, it was good. Thanks for taking me."

"Yeah it was. So, let's do it again? How about Sunday? We could see a movie and grab a bite afterwards?"

Suzie looked at him as if he was joking, but it appeared he was serious. She shrugged.

"Okay."

Neither knew what to say. Robbie ran his hands through his hair, as he did every time he saw Suzie.

"Okay, yeah, great. I'll swing by your dorm…"

Suzie watched him walk off. Her heart was beating faster than it ever had before. This guy liked her. It felt strange— and exciting at the same time. In a weird way, he made her feel safe. It was a feeling she hadn't felt for many years, since her childhood, since before the death of her father. Now, she would only experience that fleeting safety in her recurring dreams of him. They always started the same way:

The melancholic first note was struck. It lingered in the warm, sunshine-filled room. Then, a cascade of notes followed. Gentle at first, they danced and flitted as the music built, as the tempo increased, as the loneliness of the piece filled Suzie's mind.

Suzie would look up from the corner. She recognized Chopin's *Ballade Number 1*; she remembered every note, as if each one was a part of her soul. Out of the haze, she'd realize it was her father playing. He was sitting at his old piano, his hands moving, his eyes shut in concentration as he played.

She wanted to stand up, to walk over to him and place a hand on his thin shoulder. But she would risk him turning around to smile at her, and in doing so, stopping.

She watched in wonder as the blue-veined hands, so awkward in life, so unsteady and fumbling, moved like they used to, with impeccable timing, with deft assurance. The music echoed and distorted in the depths of her mind, notes bounced and reverberated, muffled at times, then louder, then softer. He played on, his head dipping toward the keys, listening intently like a bird, his head cocked to the side, utterly transfixed by the sounds; their depth, their longing.

This was always his favorite piece of music. And it was, by extension, her favorite too. Suzie recalled a moment as a child when she managed to crawl up onto his knee, squeezing herself between his lap and the piano. She wanted to get close to him, to reach the silent inner world that was his real domain, though she would not have known it as such, being so small.

She recalled that he barely registered her plump weight, her sticky hands as she climbed, clinging to his cheap suit pants, the same brown pair he wore every day to teach his students. She remembered how he continued playing this tune, unaware of her presence except as a slight distraction, like a fly buzzing against the window or a puppy nudging its nose at him to be petted. He was transported elsewhere, the world in his mind unreachable to anyone else. Even then, as a small child, she sensed he was somewhere far away.

Despite her efforts, he kept on playing, and so she settled down like a kitten on his lap, and listened, head cocked, birdlike as well, in her own childish way. They were sad sounds, sounds of beauty and yearning, sounds that told her something about her father and the world his mind inhabited that a child couldn't yet comprehend.

The music built and built, at first slowly and gracefully, then with an urgency, a complexity, that always took her off guard. Suzie wanted to touch him, to feel his presence. But she stayed where she was, barely breathing, feeling the sounds roll over her, feeling them permeate her troubled mind.

Then she'd wake up, but the sounds still rolled around in her head. They didn't behave like they did in other peoples' heads. They took over.

If you didn't count the death of her father, Suzie had by all appearances a relatively 'normal' childhood. She'd gone to school, got good grades, played with dolls, and read books until she was old enough to experience the wider world. Yet, sometimes, at night, in the moments before she fell asleep, she would experience a hazy sensation of perfume and red lips kissing her cheek. It didn't feel like a memory—as there was no one like that in her life—but it had always puzzled her, unsettled her.

She knew it was her mind that was 'wrong'—and so she would look at immaculate, elegant Dana, and wonder how on earth this graceful, quiet woman had spawned the monster that was Suzie; the erratic, mentally ill, burden. But now, there was someone at least who didn't seem to mind, who was unfazed by her strangeness.

Bang! Bang!

"Dammit, Suzie, why can't you just get ready and go out like everyone else? Why can't you be normal for once!" Andrea raged.

Then, a moment later, the dorm room door slammed shut, and Suzie heard her roommate storm out. She was still crouching in the shower as cold water ran over her body now, but she barely felt it.

One minute alone is all I want. Why don't people let me have that, at least? Suzie thought. She sighed as she moved her head downward and let the cold water run over her hair and scalp. If only it would wash away her illness. If only life was that simple, could be changed that easily. She didn't hear as the door outside opened and someone else entered the dorm room.

"Hey Suze. What're you up to? Babe, are you ok?" It was Robbie's voice. Suzie bolted upright, no longer crouching, and almost slipped.

"Babe? Come on, let's go grab a bite. You're beautiful already, you don't need to shower for hours. Come out, Suzie. Come on, let's go…"

Robbie's voice was soothing, coaxing. It seemed to break the spell. Suzie stepped out of the shower, and as she did so, she caught sight of her body under the bright light in the bathroom mirror. Her ribs showed when she breathed in. The contours of her bones were revealed as she moved. She was borderline emaciated, and this thrilled her secretly.

Suzie tried not to eat, though she had to when others began to notice. Eating a meal felt like failure, felt like yet another loss of control to Suzie, so she pushed her food around the plate, and lied about having already eaten earlier. Her counselor told her she had to eat, and had to talk about why she felt she couldn't, but to Suzie it was simple. While her mind was uncontrollable and unmanageable, her body would be her domain. She knew it wasn't healthy. She knew she should try harder, but she wouldn't. She couldn't.

Anyway, Dana always told her that a woman must be slim to attract the right man. At least, that's how Suzie remembered it. Surely, she was just following her mother's instructions, and Robbie didn't seem to mind. He didn't comment about her body, and she liked that about him. He didn't force her to eat, or talk about food at all—yet another reason she felt safe being her messed-up self with him.

"Babe?"

Tap, tap, tap. Then, the doorknob rattled.

"I'm coming. Just a second. Honestly, I'm fine. Andrea's just being a grumpy bitch… Can't believe you went and got Rob, Andrea!" Suzie shouted back through the door, unlocking it and stepping out in a towel, her long hair hanging loose down her back, dripping water on the floor.

Andrea raised her eyebrow but said nothing, instead, grabbing her wash bag and stepping into the bathroom, where she locked the door firmly. Safely inside, she yelled: "And I called your MOTHER too."

"You called MY MOTHER! Shit, Andrea! Why did you do that?" Suzie shouted.

Robbie took ahold of Suzie's shoulders gently, steering her to the bed and her pile of clothes.

"Don't look at me like that. She was worried about you, that's all… She was trying to help…" Robbie said, sitting on her bed, smiling his sweet smile.

"Help, shmelp…" Suzie muttered darkly. She looked up at Robbie, scowling at first—then she couldn't help but smile. For a moment, Suzie was dazzled by him and his relaxed manner. Why would a guy like him be attracted to her? The bad thoughts rushed back instantly, but this time she ignored them, grabbed a smaller towel and began to dry her hair.

"She had no right to do that," she said sullenly. It was Robbie's turn to raise his eyebrow.

"She's your friend and she's worried about you, like it or not. Dana is coming soon so be warned. Apparently, the college called her and said you're disrupting class. Look, just, get yourself dry and let's get out of here."

"His class disrupted my thoughts," Suzie grumbled, but before she could say more, Robbie planted a kiss on her mouth. She was suspended in time, lost in the moment, which was all too brief.

She nodded. None of this was easy, but nothing ever had been for Suzie.

Chapter 3: Suzie

The voices wouldn't stop. Every day they seemed to get louder.

Suzie didn't name them, like some people with her condition did. That was up to them. *I guess whatever makes life easier,* she would think. But, she wondered if the real reason she left them nameless was that she didn't want to acknowledge their existence, though they colored every area of her life. They were her first secrets—until they weren't. Until the noise of them drowned out everything else and she had to do what they told her.

The voices would keep up their incessant demands, until Suzie gave in, hoping her obedience would finally silence them. She often felt like an intruder in a story she didn't understand, as if she were performing her actions mechanically, someone else pulling the strings. She knew the voices hated her with a violence that surprised Suzie. The pyschs would tell her that the voices were a part of her, was her and the self-loathing that colored every aspect of Suzie's body and mind.

Back in class the next day, Suzie was trying to concentrate as the same professor droned on about something.

Literature had been Suzie's refuge growing up. She was always able to sink into a book, even if sometimes she could only manage a few lines before a myriad of thoughts, voices, and ideas slammed across her brain. But studying it at Hudson was proving even more difficult.

The professor was right. She did disrupt class. She either checked out completely, staring into space—or she became agitated, especially when other students didn't know perfectly obvious answers to perfectly obvious questions. Suzie was bright, very bright, but her brain wouldn't cooperate on demand, and so her intelligence and concentration ebbed and flowed.

One of the students asked (in Suzie's opinion) an intensely stupid question. It was Chloe, the wannabe influencer, who always seemed to be at the center of a gaggle of admirers—and always made Suzie's life as miserable as possible. Suzie couldn't fathom how someone as dim-witted as Chloe had been accepted into Hudson. *Probably screwing an admissions officer,* she thought.

Today's effort to persecute Suzie was no different. As Chloe spoke, a couple of her friends turned to face Suzie as if they knew her thoughts. They scowled and whispered together, laughed and then looked back at her.

Poisonous bitches. Poisonous bitches. Poisonous bitches. Do something now! Hurt the bitches. Hurt them—before they hurt you... Suzie tried to ignore the little girl's childish voice, but it kept on lisping the spiteful words.

Do something. They're laughing at you. Poisonous bitches! See how much they hate you!

The small child's voice was growing more and more insistent. As if sensing Suzie's vulnerability, the voice upped its game:

Chloe just wants Robbie. She wants to steal him from you. See how Robbie looks at her. She's so pretty and so popular. So unlike you, in fact... She's poison. She needs to be dealt with. She laughs at you. She hates you. She tells everyone what a freak you are. She tells everyone that Robbie only wants you out of pity and because he can't have her. She says Robbie laughs at you. Together they snigger, they laugh, they point at you...

Suzie tried to concentrate. Her hand was up as she knew what the professor wanted to hear. She knew what to say. She'd read *The Tempest,* like, a million times. If only the voice, the little girl, would shut up and leave her alone. Instead, the tempo and the volume increased and increased.

"Aghh, just stop!" Suzie let out in exasperation, and only realized she'd said this out loud because some students nearby looked over at her.

Chloe laughs at you. She's laughing at you now, everyone is. They can see your hand is up and they know how stupid you are. They know you shouldn't be here because you're such a freak. You're Robbie's pity hook-up. You're nothing, nothing, nothing—less-than-nothing. They all hate you. Look, she's looking at you. She wants to hurt you with knives. One day, she'll throw blades at you, you can see it in her eyes. She hates you, they all do. Throw the chair. Throw the chair at her. Throw the chair at that evil bitch…

The voice was louder than it had been for a long time. Perhaps the chasers she downed last night out with Robbie had messed with her brain chemistry. Perhaps she really was just a piece of shit whom everyone pitied. Suzie shook her head, couldn't remove the thoughts. They only got louder and louder, until she was holding her ears.

"Ms. Franks. Is everything okay? You look like you wanted to speak?" Professor Rami looked (for once) like he was actually concerned about her. Suzie tried to speak, but the words had all piled up and were jumbled in her mind now. Her mouth was dry, her palms sweaty. She couldn't take it anymore. She stood up, suddenly unsure. Rami stopped talking. They all stared.

Throw the fucking chair. Show that bitch what you can do. That'll stop her poisonous whispers, she won't do it again. Take that bitch out. Throw the chair. Throw the chair. Throw the chair…

Suzie finally snapped. With a strangled cry, she reached for her chair and before she knew what she was doing, she took it in her hands and with a strength she didn't know she possessed, she threw it across the hall, straight at Chloe, the doe-eyed, shiny-haired, fingers-covered-in-diamonds, grade-A bitch.

Chaos broke out, the once-muted whispers of students now erupting into a cacophony of shocked voices and panicked gasps, echoing through the lecture hall.   "Shit! What's that crazy bitch, Suzie, doing now?" someone said.

"Somebody stop her, she's freaking out!" someone else exclaimed.

Suzie darted her head around wildly as the students all scrambled for cover, expecting her to throw another missile. The professor stood shell-shocked at the front of the hall, his arms outstretched, attempting to calm her down. But his words didn't register. Just a moment ago, Chloe had been talking Shakespeare. Now, she cowered on the floor, a huddle of students around her.

Suzie's head buzzed and she realized that some of the guys had surrounded her and were looking awkwardly to each other, perhaps waiting for a cue to take her down. Suzie took advantage of their hesitation. The voices in her head were screaming now and all she knew was, she had to get out. A sob escaping from her lips, she fled, her bag slung over her shoulder, bouncing on her hip as she ran. Chloe, the class bitch, the one she had just tried to assault with a plastic chair, was surrounded by her coven, who stared open-mouthed at Suzie as she escaped.

Within hours, Suzie was found and ushered into the dean's office, a room filled with floor-to-ceiling bookshelves, a polished mahogany desk, and an atmosphere of quiet authority.

"You leave us in a very difficult position, Ms. Franks," the dean began, her voice firm yet empathetic. The dean was a serious-looking woman in her late fifties, wearing a fashionable navy-blue suit, her round glasses perched on her head.

"We understand your mental health condition, and we also understand that you are due to start a course of medication fairly soon—"

"You've spoken to Dana." It was a statement rather than a question. Of course, they'd spoken to her mother, how could they not?

"Yes, we've been in regular contact with your mother. She's very worried about you, and this… incident won't help with that. Fortunately, you missed. The student concerned received only minor injuries as she evaded the chair, and your mother has begged us not to expel you on the grounds that you have this treatment starting. But we need to be reassured that you have the support you need to be here, and we need reassurance that our students will be safe entering a classroom with you. Do you understand me?" Despite her characteristic formality, the dean wasn't being unkind, in fact, she was surprisingly calm with Suzie.

Meanwhile, all Suzie could think of was Chloe's face, that look of shock as the chair flew through the air. She shuddered at the thought of it. She could have killed her. She looked up at the dean who was leaning against her desk, standing directly in front of Suzie, and a flurry of anxious thoughts raced through her mind: Would she be expelled? If she was, what would happen next? Where would she go?

"Do you have anything to say for yourself?" the dean looked over at Suzie, who was fidgeting in her chair, pulling at a non-existent thread on her black leggings, legs crossed, arms held tightly to her body. She said nothing, and looked down at the floor.

The dean leaned forward slightly. "We want to help you, Suzie. You're a bright student. We know you can do well and we want to help you reach that potential, but you have to work with us on this too. There are pressures on you, I can't even imagine, and we pride ourselves on being an inclusive institution. We will work with you, if you, to the best of your ability, work with us…"

For a brief moment, Suzie wondered if she would say anything at all. Inside her mind, words were forming, but they weren't helpful at all.

College is dumb. Life is dumb. This is all dumb. It'd be better if I left…

The image of Dana flashed suddenly through Suzie's mind. Her mother would sigh right about now, turn to her, and say something like 'you have to face reality'—but what *was* reality? And how could she go about facing it when her brain was always playing tricks on her?

Suzie shrugged. "I guess I'll take the meds."

She hadn't expected to say that, but then again she hadn't expected to throw a chair at anyone today.

"That's good to hear, Ms. Franks. Let's talk about what that will mean, both for you and the university…"

Finally, the terms were agreed to. Suzie would attend counseling sessions at least once a week, and would begin taking medication once the proper assessments had been done, something Suzie had consistently refused until now. In return, she wouldn't be expelled— at least not yet.

Robbie was waiting outside the office when she walked out. Tears streamed down her face, leaving hot trails on her cheeks, while her shoulders slumped and her eyelids grew heavy, a deep exhaustion settling into her bones.

"You got her good." Robbie smiled, making light of it in an effort to cheer her up. Though he hadn't yet seen it for himself, they both knew the torment delivered to Suzie on a daily basis from Chloe and her gang. They both knew Suzie was one more incident away from expulsion, but in that moment, he made her smile. Suzie didn't smile often—except when she was with him.

That night, unable to find solace in sleep, she crept out of the dorm room to light a cigarette and breathe it out into the crisp autumn air. None of it made sense. None of it ever made sense. Exhaling, she ground the cigarette butt into a patch of damp grass, and ventured back inside.

It was then that she pulled a water bottle out of her dresser and took a generous swig of the clear liquid inside. She felt the tension begin to subside, as if the voices were washed away for now. Vodka seemed to have that effect lately. Suzie hoped it would last.

Chapter 4: Dana

"Suzie."

Mom sometimes had a way of saying her name that made it sound like a complete and utter reproval of all things Suzie. This was one of those times.

"Behave or leave, that's what they're saying at Hudson now, honey. Get help or go somewhere else to continue your education… You disrupt class, regularly. This can't continue." Dana's eyes were fixed on the road as they drove. Suzie wasn't sure where they were going. She'd zoned out when her mother told her, but it didn't matter anyway. Suzie didn't care, at least outwardly. She chewed gum, her mind racing, her thoughts scattered. She knew she was in trouble, but then again, wasn't she always?

"That isn't what the dean said, Mom. She said as long as I was able to work with them, I could stay, and that's what I'm doing… Anyway, Rami's classes disrupt my thoughts. Like I care what Professor Rami thinks. His classes are boring, and obvious. I. Can't. Stand. The. Boredom." Suzie stared out the window. "And how does this prepare me for the real world? The only thing like school in real life is prison…"

"Suzanne, are you even listening? Am I talking to myself again?" Dana said as she drove. She felt the same sense of frustration, anger, the desperate unfairness she always felt when she was trying to get through to the young woman. Dana would never say this to Suzanne, but sometimes she wished her daughter were 'normal,' just like everyone else— able to talk, reason, and act like an adult. Sometimes, dealing with someone with a mental illness was just too hard, just too much to ask of her.

Being a single parent was difficult enough, even without a condition that was so hard on the young girl she cared for. Dana worked as an accountant for a local family-run chain of coffee shops, so she had a regular income, which was more than many single moms had. Even so, she was still left bringing up a troubled young girl alone, trying to map out the best possible future for her, but feeling overwhelmed much of the time.

It was always one step forward and two steps back. So many doctor appointments, paramedics, healthcare professionals, then psychiatrists, therapists, and now college counselors. So much of Dana's time and energy had gone into trying to help Suzanne over the years, so much time that never really seemed to move either of them forward.

"Suzanne, honestly, I really need you to listen. I know it's hard for you. I have no idea what it's like to be you, to have the struggles you have, but there is a way out. The medication will help you, and it's time you started taking it. I know you've agreed to, but saying something in the dean's office to avoid expulsion is very different to actually doing it…

"It's an easy choice now, honey. If you don't take it, they'll probably ask you to leave. They're worried you're a danger to yourself—and to others too."

"Yeah, I know this, Mom. For God's sake, give me a break," Suzie said. "I never wanted to go to college in the first place."

Neither of them spoke for a long time. Suzie was being unfair here, and Dana resented it. True, Suzanne had been nervous, even unwilling, to attend college, but Dana saw it as a vital first step toward independence, and a life of her own. She had met with enough doctors over the years to know that a 'normal' life was possible for Suzanne, with the right medication and support. Even so, she'd been apprehensive. How would Suzanne cope with living in a dorm? How would she handle the complexities of friendships and relationships? How would she manage the workload?

Suzanne's acceptance at Hudson as an English major had marked a considerable success. For a moment, Dana felt she could finally breathe again. Was there finally a glimmer of hope for Suzanne? Perhaps she had a future outside the bleak lighting of the hospital, as her arms were patched up again, as the scars were covered, as the episodes of self-harming exploded their lives like a bomb detonating each time.

By now the initial elation of Suzie's college acceptance had vanished, leaving behind that usual sick feeling in Dana's stomach, the terrible, shameful feeling she had that really, she wished the young woman sitting next to her hadn't been born. Or worse, that she—Dana—was really the one to blame for Suzanne's illness. Dana hated herself for these feelings, but they'd persisted over the years and now they seemed written into her DNA.

"I never know what's going on in my brain, can't you see that, Mom?"

"Of course, honey. I don't want to fight. I want to support you, but you need to help me too."

The car tires crunched on gravel, sending small stones scattering as they pulled off the highway and into the parking lot of a roadside café. Inside, they sat together in a booth by the window—though it felt like they were worlds apart. Outside, a fine drizzle was settling over the highway as autumn crept in, though it was still mild.

"Cream soda. Nothing to eat, I'm not hungry," Suzie said, eying the menu.

Dana couldn't help herself, she sighed again. When would she eat? When would she look after herself? If only Suzanne could see herself through Dana's eyes. She was pale and skinny. Her eyes looked drawn and it was clear she was not getting enough sleep, not eating properly, and yet there was so much potential.

"Suzie, you're a beautiful girl," Dana began, noting her daughter's big blue eyes, jet black hair that hung down her back and her wiry, athletic frame. "And you're smart. You're a capable young woman, despite dealing with the challenges you do…" If only Suzie could see herself as Dana saw her, it would make all the difference.

Before Suzie had time to respond, the waitress came over, and Dana asked for a club salad and herbal tea, hoping Suzanne would follow suit. Suzie looked away and Dana knew the battle was over on that subject before it had even begun.

"Look, Suzanne, we know you struggle. I'd do anything in my power to help you, but you won't let me. You never let me help…" Dana's voice trembled as she spoke. "Your professors say you're defiant in class, you won't listen, you walk out of lectures. You threw a chair, for heaven's sake! How can they teach you, if you act like that? What'll happen to you if you don't get help? You need help—and help is there for you…"

Suzie was lost in her thoughts, as the waitress brought Dana her salad and the glass containing the cream soda was set in front of her. Suzie felt a sudden urge to swipe the glass from the table and watch it shatter on the floor, a fitting representation of her mind.

"Suzanne, are you listening? Honey, we need to get you help. When we get back to Hudson, you're scheduled to see the psychiatrist who's going to start you on the medication you need. There's really no other way, honey. It's for your own good, you can see that, can't you?"

Suzie said nothing, merely staring at her cream soda, wondering if she should obey the voices and dash it to the floor.

"It's time for you to face up to your condition and accept help," Dana continued firmly. "It's becoming harder and harder to justify your enrollment at Hudson when you keep refusing medication. With the right treatment, you can live a normal life. Wouldn't you like that?"

Suzie looked over at her. Eventually she spoke.

"But, what's normal, Mom?"

Some days she thought Dana was out to destroy her, to make her submissive and pliable. Other days, she believed in her mother and felt things would be okay. Suzie let out a long breath. She could see she had no choice now. Maybe the meds would help.

Suzie nodded her assent. "Fine."

Dana appeared satisfied. She smiled at Suzie, who dropped her gaze, sucked on her straw as the bubbling sweet soda bit at her tongue.

They finished and Dana paid. The drive back was silent as they both kept to their own thoughts. Dana dropped Suzie back at her dorm, yet still they said nothing except a terse goodbye. Suzie's gaze lingered on the receding taillights of her mother's car, the distance between them growing with each passing moment. She was unsure how she felt, unsure about everything.

Chapter 5: Chit-Chat

"Listen, I'm just here for the medication. Can we skip the chit-chat?" Suzie asked Dr. Fedowski, the university psychiatrist.

"Unfortunately, the State of Oregon does require the chit-chat first," he responded, looking up from his notes with a wry smile. "I see you've had some problems with inattention, hallucinations, and some chaotic and, even violent behavior. Would that sound like a fair assessment to you?"

"I see things that aren't there," she said tersely, picking at a piece of fluff on the hem of her mini skirt. She was wearing thick black leggings and Doc Martens boots, though the day was mild.

"Okay, so tell me more," Dr. Fedowski encouraged gently, leaning back in his worn leather chair. The late afternoon sunlight filtered through the blinds, casting striped patterns across his face. He held a pen, and Suzie winced as he began taking down a few notes. *Scratch. Scratch*, went the pen.

"Um, well I have schizophrenia, so I know there's something weird going on in my brain. I'm not normal." Suzie attempted a laugh but the sound came out as a strangled croak.

"Good, uh huh, go on…"

Suzie looked over at a poster on the wall that read, "Today is a good day!" She could laugh at that, but things didn't feel very funny these days. Robbie had urged Suzie to attend this, her first appointment since the chair throwing incident. He was pretty brutal, telling her it was this way or no way.

"Suze, you've got to do this or they'll kick you out. And hey, babe, I don't mean to upset you but you do need help.

Throwing a chair isn't the best way to make friends and influence people." He grinned.

Suzie and Robbie had been lying under a tree in the lush green grass on campus, waiting for the next lecture after lunch, when he'd sat up, picked a tendril of her hair and stroked his hand through it.

"How do I know they're not trying to control me?' Suzie asked, drawing her knees up to her chest. The voices were loud that day. They were telling her to do stuff again, hurt her arm again, throw *something*.

"Babe, that's your illness talking. The psychs know what they're doing—and if it's the only way you can stay here then it's got to be worth a shot, right?"

Suzie nodded, a sense of bleakness settling over her. For years, her mother had urged her to seek help, but somehow it felt better coming from her boyfriend. She was able to listen to him in a way she just couldn't with Dana.

"I just wish the voices would stop. I just wish I was normal…" she said sadly.

Robbie laughed. "Babe, I'd hate you being normal! That's the dumbest thing I've ever heard. And the voices, well, the meds'll take the edge off those, right? Worth a shot?"

Suzie looked at him, and nodded. "I'll give it a shot," she agreed reluctantly.

So, here she was, sitting in front of the college psychiatrist, spilling her guts so she could be assessed and medicated, so she could finally fit in and be 'normal'. Wasn't that what she'd always wanted? Now that Suzie was here, she wasn't sure anymore.

"I think when I threw the chair, it was like a way of stopping the voices as much as those bitches in class. I don't really know why I do things. The voices in my head get really loud, they're really on me all the time, and sometimes I just crack. I go mental and do stupid things. I felt better afterwards though…"

The psychiatrist looked up from his notes at her.

"Look, I'm not a psycho. I don't want to hurt people—well, not other people. I hurt myself when it gets too much. When I cut my arm, it stops the raging inside me, and it means I don't throw anything or hurt anyone else. It feels safer, I guess, though the feelings always come back."

"I see, and so in a way, it's a pattern of behavior that is actually trying to protect other people from what is going on in your mind, when the pressure builds up and the voices get too much for you?"

"Yes, that's exactly it!"

"So we haven't talked about the medication yet, but I'm going to prescribe a low dose of Olanzapine. It's one of the newer medications, and it can be really helpful in balancing out your brain chemistry. It makes hallucinations such as the ones you describe, less likely, and it also helps with depression and the low moods. Obviously, it's not a good idea to mix any prescribed medication with alcohol or illegal drugs. And also marijuana. Do you have any questions?" The psychiatrist was already reaching for his prescription pad and writing out the dose.

Moments later, Suzie walked out, though not triumphantly, prescription in hand. As expected, Robbie was waiting patiently outside, and offering her a reassuring smile.

"Okay, so let's go and get that now, before you change your mind." He reached over and kissed her forehead.

Suzie still couldn't believe they were an item. They were still dating, and it was now generally accepted on campus that they were together, though quite the odd couple. Robbie, the quintessential jock, with blond hair and a permanent tan, alongside Suzie with her black hair, pale skin and blue eyes. When he grinned at her, she found it hard to inhale. Suzie sunk a little into his arms, before they walked out together, toward the pharmacy, and the beginning of treatment.

Chapter 6: Love

Suzie took the medication. Within days, something felt different. Within a few weeks, the voices were receding, like the sounds of a babbling brook as one moved further away. Already, she felt calmer, able to concentrate, but there was one thing she'd noticed which unsettled her. She was putting on weight.

"Suze, you look gorgeous. It looks good on you, I promise," Robbie said, kissing her forehead as they lay on the hood of his Mustang, the glossy, deep-red paint reflecting the moonlight. Fall had turned to winter now, and they were wrapped in blankets, their breath misty flumes in the light from the headlamps, as they lay gazing at the stars.

Suzie looked up at him. She was in his arms, trying to figure out how she could possibly explain a lifetime's troubled relationship with her body to someone so evidently at ease with himself.

In some ways, Rob was a simple soul. He was loyal. He looked out for her. He was steady in a way she wasn't, and not for the first time, she wondered how he'd gotten to be like that. What went right for him that didn't for her? She'd asked him before, about his family and growing up, knowing she was asking in a forensic way, trying to figure it out.

He'd shrugged and said: "It wasn't anything special. There was Mom, Dad, and my three sisters. It was a pretty regular life."

Suzie had stared at him, and the way he brushed off 'regular' like it wasn't anything special. Like it wasn't unusual, and mind-bendingly fragile and extraordinary.

"And so, what do your sisters do? Did you get along? What was it like having sisters and no brothers?" Suzie's questions poured out. She was fascinated by the ease of his life —an ease he wore draped over his broad shoulders without him even knowing.

"Mostly it was good, but one of my sisters, Melissa, got sick, really sick. We had to spend a lot of time in hospitals and driving around the state to take her to different specialists. A lot of it I don't remember, but I do remember Mom telling us how bad Melissa was, and that she might not survive." Robbie paused before continuing. "She got better but we always worried about her. I still do, if I'm honest. That never goes away even though we're grown-up now," he'd said, with a candor that made Suzie's heart contract.

Sometimes when she felt a strong emotion, like at moments like these, she would find herself being pulled back into painful childhood memories. There was one she kept revisiting. It was the crux of her life, the moment when she realized her father wasn't coming home, when she felt the visceral pain of his death.

She was eight years old. It was a fresh spring day, the air warm, the sun shining in the blue sky, or so she remembered. She walked in the house, her backpack slung over her shoulder. She took a breath. The air smelled of furniture polish and spring. Suzie dropped her backpack and wandered into the office, Dana's usual location at this time, but no one was there. Confused, she headed upstairs, and it wasn't until she got to the top that she heard the sound, a sound that still reverberated in her mind sometimes.

It was her mother crying. Suzie froze for a moment, wondering what was going on, then she edged toward her parents' bedroom. The door was ajar, and Suzie could see what looked like Dana, prostrate on the bed. Utterly baffled now, Suzie tried to back off, but as she did so, the floorboards creaked, and Dana looked up. Her face was red and blotchy, her eyes rimmed with tears.

"Oh honey, I didn't hear you come in. I'm sorry. I'm so sorry…" Dana's voice was croaky, as if she had a cold.

Suzie stared back at her, feeling uncertain. What was she supposed to do? This was all so unfamiliar, so strange. Should she comfort her? What was wrong anyway? It had to be bad for her mommy to be so distraught.

"Come and sit with me, Suzanne. I have something I need to tell you and it's so hard, it's so hard." Dana began to cry again. Suzie wanted to bolt away. This was way too much, way out of her comfort zone.

"Listen, honey. It's your dad. I don't know how to tell you. I'm not sure I can find the right words, but he's gone. Oh, Suzanne… he's dead, my love, he's dead. He won't be coming home to us again. He had a heart attack at work. They rushed him to the hospital, but it was too late. He didn't suffer, no, not at all. He went so quickly, like the angel he was. He was just here with us on this earth one minute, and then he wasn't…"

Suzie had stared at her mother, not quite understanding her words. Something inside her felt like it broke in that moment, something that was unrepairable. The next thing she knew, she was running outside, away from the house.

At the end of the road, she stopped, as cars zipped past, as other kids walked home, back to their ordinary lives where tragedies like this never happened. Suzie stared around wildly, not knowing where to go or what to do. And then it hit her like a truck. Daddy was dead.

"You were lucky," she said to Robbie simply, remembering where she was, remembering that that moment had passed long ago. "I don't mean your sister was lucky. I'm sorry to hear about her illness, that must've been tough, but you were a big family and all together. That must've been nice…"

The air was cold, but Suzie felt warm laying next to Robbie on the hood, though she felt unsettled. The waistband of her jeans was digging into her stomach, and the sensation was unpleasant.

As time had gone by, and as the meds started to work and made her so hungry all of a sudden, her body had begun to change—and she did not like it at all. She'd known she was putting on weight for a few weeks. She saw it creep silently and slowly onto her slim frame, and with it came a growing sense of panic. She felt trapped.

She'd spent even more time in the shower under the cold water, trying to melt the 'fat' away; shivering and staring into that damn mirror. Suzie hated the sensation that she was growing, expanding.

She felt out of control now, though the fragments of her brain felt more stitched together. It seemed unfair to her that while her brain was settling and she was able to concentrate in class, that this new part of her treatment had bubbled up these feelings of self-loathing that she'd tried to suppress for so long. Robbie noticed, as he always did.

"Babe, you don't need to cover up," he'd said lazily, watching her pile on layers of clothes. Yes, it was getting cold, but he knew something was up. He'd watched Suzie as she'd begun taking her medication, amazed that she was actually doing it, feeling proud of her and her resilience. He guessed she'd had an unhappy start in life, though they didn't talk too much about that.

She'd said her father had died when she was young but seemed reluctant to say more, so Robbie never pushed it. He likened being with Suzie to caring for a horse. You had to let her come to you. If you tried to force her with anything, she'd bolt. She always seemed on the verge of bolting. That's why he was always careful around her, gentle. She seemed unused to tenderness.

"I love you, you know," Robbie said, making his girlfriend blush and look away. "I know I've told you before, but I really do love you," Robbie said, pulling a blanket over Suzie's legs which were molded into the shape of his body as they lay there. He tucked a length of long black hair behind Suzie's ear, and gazed into her eyes.

Suzie looked up at him. "I...I..." she started, but Robbie grinned and leaned down to kiss her.

"Don't worry. We don't need words. I know what you mean." He smiled, making Suzie blush again.

He held up the blunt he'd painstakingly rolled while balancing on the hood, and lit it, drawing the smoke deep into his lungs. Suzie watched him, fascinated. She'd been using alcohol to get high, to try to block out the crazy in her head, but she'd always been scared of weed. Didn't they say that made you crazy too? Something to do with messing up your brain chemicals?

Before she could think any further, she saw Robbie's face relax, saw him roll his eyes back, shut them and lay back, and she reached out to take the blunt from his hand.

"You sure, babe? Thought you didn't do blunts?" Robbie arched an eyebrow but failed to lift his head. "Man, the stars are *amaaaaaazing* tonight. Look at that one, babe, it's so bright."

Suzie giggled. Robbie was always so cute when he was high. She wanted to be cute too.

"I want to try. How bad could it be? You do okay and you're always stoned." she giggled again, making Robbie laugh out loud.

She held the blunt to her lips and inhaled. The smoke hit the back of her throat with a burning sensation, and she choked and spluttered.

Robbie sat up now. "Jeez, you scared me. At least do it right. Just a small toke, like this. Watch…" He smoothly drew in the smoke, held it for a few seconds, smiled, then let the smoke out in a long exhalation.

"Go on, you try now…" he said, handing it back.

Suzie smiled. Already she felt a warm sensation, a feeling of lightness and relaxation starting to seep under her skin. She tried again. This time, it was smooth, and so she took another, then another inhalation.

Robbie took it back from her and smiled as she sunk down into the crook of his arm. She knew she was stressing about something but couldn't remember it now. It was something about her body, but now her body felt great! She smiled, the sky seemed to twinkle just above her head as the effect of the cannabis took hold.

"Oh my God, the stars. They look incredible. So beautiful…"

"Just like you," Robbie added, turning onto one elbow. He touched her face with one hand, brushed her hair. "I love you" he offered again.

"I love you too. Always," she said, eventually, staring into Robbie's eyes. Something about the weed made her feel free, wild perhaps, and she discovered she liked it. Perhaps she'd found a way to make everything okay, to make her bad thoughts disappear. Perhaps, finally, Suzie could be free.

Chapter 7: Spiraling Down

"Babe… Babe? I've been calling you. You're not answering? I've been worried." Robbie was standing outside, peering through the cracked doorway into Suzie's dorm room. Suzie's hair clung to her face in tangled disarray, and her bloodshot eyes squinted against the intruding light as she opened the door further.

"What time is it?" was all she could manage, turning her back on him and staggering back into bed. It was obvious it was way past morning, as the winter sun had started to set, casting an orange glow around the room. Andrea's bed was empty and had been made, the comforter smoothed down, the pillows fluffed up, and her childhood teddy bear sitting in its usual place. Suzie's side of the room, by contrast, was a mess. Her bed was disheveled, and there were cups and plates with half-eaten meals around her.

"You weren't in any classes today, and I've tried calling you and texting. What's going on? Babe, it stinks of weed in here!" Robbie said, his voice rising in exasperation as he flung open the window, letting a gust of frigid air rush in and collide with the heavy stench of marijuana smoke. "How much have you been smoking? I only gave you what I had because you said it helped you sleep… They'll kick you out if they smell this in the hall!"

Suzie frowned. "It does help me sleep. You can stop lecturing me though. You sound like my mother." She pulled the covers back over herself and settled back in.

It was Robbie's turn to frown. "Woah, stop right there. I'm definitely not your mother! And hey, where's the rest of the weed? I gave you a lot last night. It was supposed to last all week."

Suzie said nothing. She wished that Robbie would just go away. Her head was pounding, her throat parched. She could tell a headache was imminent, and she still felt unsteady. He'd soon realize she smoked all of it overnight.

She vaguely remembered Andrea storming out—but not before making her bed like the good girl she was—to go and stay in another friend's dorm because she couldn't sleep with the fog of all the strong-smelling smoke. *Good riddance,* Suzie had thought. She knew, deep down, she had done something wrong, but she felt like shit and there was a strange buzzing sensation in her head.

"I don't know. Maybe Andrea took it?' she lied, hoping he'd go easy on her. "Why don't you get in with me and we'll chill here together?"

Robbie sat down heavily on the bed, sighing. "Listen, it's my fault. I should never have let you have that first blunt. That was weeks ago though, and you're smoking more than me and my friends combined.

"Honestly, it's not good for you. You're missing class and everyone is saying you'll fail this semester. Things were going good for you, babe. Come on. Get dressed and you can at least catch the end of the last lecture…"

Robbie's voice was soft now, beguiling. Suzie nestled further down into the warmth of the comforter. She felt like doing jack shit today, just nursing her hangover from the night, and early morning, spent smoking and listening to music. Alcohol had been her thing, until now. It calmed her down—at first anyway—and made her feel like a 'normal' person, less socially awkward and able to be with other people. But then she started getting out of control and making a fool of herself, getting too drunk, too fast and generally being too problematic, even by college standards.

Now that she'd discovered cannabis, she realized this was how she wanted to spend her time: weed, music, and Robbie, and nothing else. Except Robbie had stopped wanting to do this with her and was studying hard now.

"You need to stop, Suzie. Things are hard enough for you without throwing weed into it. You're on heavy medication. You've been much better, but now you're at risk of throwing it all away… You don't know what the effect of mixing the two could be."

Suzie put the comforter over her head so the words couldn't settle into her brain. What Robbie—and the university—did not know was that Suzie had already stopped taking her schizophrenia medication weeks ago.

She couldn't bear the thought of gaining more weight. She hated seeing herself in the mirror, and so, one day, without telling a soul, she flushed the pills down the toilet, watching them spin for a brief moment before they disappeared down the drain. She felt a dubious sense of control, like she was finally making her own decisions, living life on her own terms.

She replaced the pills with vitamin tablets so no one would guess. Almost instantly the cravings for food stopped, and Suzie felt like she could exhale again. This didn't last for long. Soon, the voices began to come back, the paranoia returned, the fears and hallucinations slid back in so that now, she smoked weed to try and dampen them down, hoping no one would guess what she'd done.

"Suzie?" Robbie sounded impatient now. The last thing she wanted to do was push away the only real friend she had, but she couldn't seem to help herself. The buzzing got louder and louder. Suzie put her hand over her ears. Robbie pulled back the comforter a little and saw her doing this. He assumed she was trying to block out his voice, so he got up and headed back to the door, his frustration evident.

"Babe, I'll check on you later. Make sure you eat something," he said, dully. The door shut with a click. Suzie stayed where she was; in the dark and heat of the comforter, wondering when he'd finally leave her too, just like her father, just like every friend she'd ever had. Why couldn't she keep her shit together? Why was life so goddamn difficult? Little did she know it was about to get even worse.

"Ms. Franks. I'm disappointed to see you back here. What happened this time?" The dean looked steadily over at Suzie as she stood opposite her desk, back in that office, back in trouble. It was like a pattern that wouldn't stop repeating.

Suzie refused to sit down. She didn't speak, couldn't speak actually. Her head felt stranger than ever. It twisted and turned and festered. Thoughts seemed to go stale. They built up and up until she exploded and did something stupid again, which was why she was here. This time, she slapped Chloe. She could almost hear the sharp impact of her palm on Chloe's cheek, echoing in her brain.

"I'm sorry. I didn't mean to do it. It just sort-of happened," Suzie mumbled. She looked down and realized she'd been wearing the same pair of leggings for a few days, and they looked unwashed.

"What happened, Ms. Franks?" the ever-formal dean asked, quietly.

"She walked up to me in the cafeteria…" Suzie didn't add that Chloe was with her coven of witches. She didn't say that she hated them all. "Chloe kinda came straight up to me like she'd been waiting for me to get there, then she just stood in front of me and wouldn't move away."

The dean frowned. "I can see how that would feel intimidating, and I will talk to Ms. Williams about it. Go on…"

"I asked what she wanted, and by then there were others sort-of gathering around us. They realized something was going down…"

At the time, Suzie had looked around for anyone who might help, but Robbie was out playing soccer with the guys and Andrea was studying in the library. Suzie had realized she was alone, in the corner of the dining hall, holding a tray containing a small salad and her usual black coffee.

"So, Chloe didn't say anything so I asked her again what she wanted…"

Suzie didn't say that this time, she asked slowly, as if that bitch Chloe was a total dumbass, which, of course, she was. Suzie also chose to omit that Chloe then narrowed her eyes, and smirked as she spoke:

"Did you know Robbie was chatting it up with Amelie last night? We think he's got a thing for her. She's curvy and pretty—so unlike you…"

Suzie withheld how Chloe's coven sniggered, making her blood boil. She also neglected to add that as her temper surged, the young schoolgirls reappeared, taunting and jeering from the room's center, their pigtails and childish attire a stark contrast to the surrounding college students.

"She said some stuff about my boyfriend," Suzie informed the dean.

That covered it, pretty much.

What Suzie could have told the dean was that by now, in the café-fearia, she was wondering if any of this was real. The room seemed to swim. They could have taunted her about anything, her bad grades, her lack of friends, her awkward manner, her uncool clothes, anything—except for Robbie. He was sacrosanct. He was the only person she had in the world, or so it seemed at times. And now, he'd been chatting up another girl on a night out that Suzie had missed because she wanted to stay in bed, smoking blunts.

"I told Chloe she was lying." Suzie shrugged. "And they all laughed…"

Suzie didn't say that some of those who'd gathered now walked off, and that someone said: "Leave her alone, she's not well…"

She didn't say that Chloe did not leave Suzie alone. She continued baiting her, telling her what a great party it was, and how *close* Robbie seemed to be with Amelie, when all of a sudden, the tray slipped from Suzie's grasp, her body seemingly beyond her control.

In an instant, her right hand shot up, and she heard the crack of the impact as her palm collided with Chloe's picture-perfect face. For a brief moment everything was quiet, then the whole place seemed to erupt. Shocked faces. People laughing. Others whistling. No one could believe Suzie had just slapped Chloe right there, in front of everyone.

She skipped telling the dean about Chloe's reaction, which went something like: "Oh my God! You fucking psycho! You psycho bitch, what's your fucking problem?" after which her friends all joined in.

Suzie chose not to tell the dean that she stood stock still after that, in shock, unable to process what she'd just done, but knowing she was in deep shit now. She chose not to add that slapping Chloe was probably one of her 'Ritalin decisions,' a term she coined to describe her rash, impulsive actions under the drug's influence.

Those were the unfortunate side effects that that particular drug had on her. Practically everyone at Hudson seemed to rely on Adderall to stay up late at night studying, but Suzie had come to prefer its cousin Ritalin for her pick-me-ups.

"What? I wasn't hitting on anyone. Suzie, don't listen to her. She's poison, just like you said. She saw me talking to Amelie. We're taking the same class together and she's nice. She's a friend, that's it," Robbie had insisted later.

"Then, why did she say that? Why do people think you were trying to get with her?" Suzie said eventually, looking at Robbie.

"Jeez, you look like shit, Suzie. That's it! No more weed. You're messing up your life, can't you see that?"

Robbie's furrowed brow and clenched fists betrayed his anger, but beneath the surface, his heart ached with worry for Suzie's well-being, a well-being he feared he'd endangered by introducing her to marijuana.

"You just got yourself into a whole lot of new trouble, Suzie. Why did you do that? Can't you just ignore her?" Robbie's face showed his disappointment in her, something Suzie couldn't bear to see.

Her lips quivered and her eyes glistened as a single tear escaped, trailing down her cheek. She shook her head.

"I can't seem to stop myself. She was saying horrible things, making me suspicious of you. I can't lose you, Robbie, I can't. I don't know what I'd do…" Her hands trembled as she tried to hold back the sobs.

"So, they said things about your boyfriend, Ms. Franks?" the dean inquired.

"Yeah. So… I hit her…"

The dean nodded. "You certainly did, Suzanne, and in doing so, you've put me in a very difficult position. Ms. Williams' parents have gotten involved. They are extremely concerned about the impact your condition is having on those around you. But I'm also concerned about some of the conduct you say you've encountered here at Hudson. I'll speak to

Ms. Williams, and I'll speak to the university counseling team. We will speak again, Ms. Franks, and very soon."

Suzie got up uneasily, finally realizing that was her dismissal, and walked from the room.

As Suzie stepped outside, she found Robbie waiting. Tears welled up in Suzie's eyes once more, and Robbie, sensing her distress, gently guided her back to the relative sanctuary of her dorm room, where a concerned Andrea awaited their arrival.

"Shit, what did you do? What happened?" She leapt up off her bed where her textbooks and papers were all spread out.

"Nothing, it was just a misunderstanding," Robbie said, then mouthed the word 'Chloe'.

Andrea nodded. "What should we do?" she said to Robbie as he led his girlfriend inside.

Suzie gripped her head tightly, curling up on her bed with her knees drawn to her chest, the worn soles of her boots leaving faint traces on the soft comforter.

"She just needs to calm down, then we'll talk."

Gently coaxing Suzie, they handed her a cup of coffee and urged her to nibble on a few bites of Andrea's sandwich.

Suzie declined their offers with a shake of her head. She began to rock gently back and forth, resting her head on her knees while Robbie's comforting arm encircled her.

"So, what happens next?" Andrea asked, sitting down next to them and gently grasping Suzie's hand. The three of them looked at each other.

"Later, when Suzie's settled down more, we call her mom," Robbie said grimly.

Chapter 8: Leaving

It didn't take long for Dana to arrive. She'd been at dinner with friends, enjoying a rare night out. Halfway through her roasted salmon, she received the desperate call.

"Mrs. Franks? I'm sorry to call you so late, but Suzie, well, she's…" Robbie's voice trailed off. What could he say? She assaulted a fellow student? She's probably going to be expelled?

"Yes, I know. They've asked me to come in tomorrow to discuss Suzie's future on campus." As politely as she could in the moment, Dana waved away the waiter who was hovering with a plate of mashed potatoes glistening in melted butter.

"Oh, okay, so they called you. She's really not doing well, Mrs. Franks. She won't stop crying. She says she's going to run away and that she'd be better off dead…"

"I'm on my way," Dana said, ending the call. She bolted up from the table. Sporting an elegant navy dress, her hair wound back in her usual chignon, she grabbed her coat and bag, apologized to her friends, and power-walked out to the car. She would've liked to throw off her heels and run, though she was unsure if it would be in the direction of the university and Suzie, or in the opposite direction—to anywhere else.

She started the car, and it bolted out of the parking lot and onto the highway.

When Dana arrived, Robbie stood nervously beneath a towering oak tree outside the freshly painted residential hall.

"I'm so sorry, I didn't know what else to do," he said sheepishly, seeing her outfit and guessing he'd just interrupted significant plans.

"It doesn't matter, young man. Suzanne is lucky to have you looking out for her. Where is she?" With a determined stride, Dana entered the bustling dormitory, her heels clicking authoritatively against the polished tile floor.

"She's with Andrea. I couldn't leave her on her own. We've both been with her all afternoon. Something's different. Something's changed again, and she's back to her old self…"

In the room, Dana walked in and went straight to Suzie. She lay sprawled across her rumpled bed, her tear-streaked face buried in the floral-patterned pillow.

"Honey… what's all this?" she said softly, picking up her hand and stroking it, just as she did when Suzie was a little girl.

"They want to hurt me," Suzie said, "they all want me to die…"

Dana looked over at Robbie, who appeared to be losing his paticncc.

"What do you mean, honey? No one wants to hurt you…"

Suzie looked up and wondered if she was hallucinating. Her mom was sitting next to her, holding her hand. Was she a child again? What was happening? Everything felt so hazy and yet sharp at the same time.

"How are you feeling?' Dana asked, not sure where to begin. "How are the meds going? Should we ask the doctor about changing your prescription? I don't want to upset you, but it seems like they're not working…"

Suzie looked to be on the verge of losing it completely. Her hands trembled violently, and her breathing came in quick, shallow gasps. Her eyes darted around the room. When she'd left the dean's office, she suddenly felt like her whole world was collapsing—or was about to collapse. Then, the thoughts started again.

Have I lost Robbie? Is he lying to me now? Was Chloe right, and I'm being naïve and stupid in believing him? I'm such a loser. I wouldn't blame him if he wanted one of the popular girls…

The thought of losing her boyfriend was too much. The buzzing in her ears was strong. That pressure in her mind felt like it was building up again. Luckily, she managed to save a ring pull from a can of soda, knowing she'd use it later, drawing it across her arm where all the other scars and lines crisscross, watching the blood, hot and red, run down her skin.

Maybe this time she should go for the artery. Maybe she really would be better off dead. That way, Robbie could have a normal girlfriend and her mom could move on with her life rather than having to bail out her lunatic daughter over and over. Maybe life was just too hard for people like her.

"Are you even taking the meds, Suze?" Robbie asked when the young woman stayed silent.

The words danced and weaved around her head. *They know*, Suzie thought. *They know everything about me… They must be watching…*

"I was always worried about how you'd cope, being away from home where you felt comfortable, well as much as you can, honey." Dana spoke now. "Suzie, why don't you come home and we'll figure this out. Maybe I was wrong insisting you try college right now."

Since she'd stopped taking her medication, Suzie had been crawling into this deep, dark hole for weeks now. Even though she was sick—she knew she needed help—she'd been looking for it in all the wrong places. One of the guys on campus had been giving her cocaine and Ritalin. She'd take anything right now to dull the noises and the overwhelming fear, the strange visions, and the paranoia.

She'd even wondered if she should go back on her schizophrenia meds, but the thought of putting weight back on, of feeling so unlike herself, of losing control, stopped her. She hadn't communicated any of this to Dana or Robbie, or anyone else. She thought they wouldn't understand. She knew they would force her back on the medication. Her brain twisted and turned. It exhausted her. If only she could stay under this comforter, warm and safe, forever.

Only a crazy person would say that, she thought. Her mother was still looking at her. With a jolt, Suzie realized she was expecting an answer.

She shook her head. If she went home, that would be it, she imagined. Her life would be over. She'd be a failure. She'd have proved to everybody that she was the loser they'd all thought she was. If she went home, she'd have to live with Dana's disappointment forever, and she knew she couldn't do that.

"I'm not going home. I'll get up. I'll see the psych. I'll do it all, Mom. Just please don't let them kick me out…"

"Suzanne, it wouldn't be a case of kicking you out but of finding out where you'd be safe, to protect you. Now, why don't you get up and take a shower while I change your bedding. This all needs a good wash, and soon we'll have you feeling better again."

Suzie didn't see the looks exchanged by Dana, Robbie, and Andrea. She didn't see the fear on all their faces.

There were bright lights and unfamiliar sounds. A doctor stood over her, flashing something into the back of her eyes.

"What's going on?" Suzie moaned, trying to get up, but realizing she couldn't move. Her body wouldn't respond, and anyway, there were tubes coming out of her arm.

"You overdosed, Suzie," Dana said, her eyes red from crying as she sat by the hospital bed. Robbie was there too. He looked uncomfortable. He kept glancing away as if Suzie was too horrible to look at, as if he were wondering if it might be time to cut his losses and finally extricate himself from her life and problems.

"What happened?" Suzie croaked. Her throat felt dry. "Give me water, please, Mom…"

Dana reached over to pour out a small cup of water from a plastic jug on the bedside table. As she did, she spoke.

"We almost lost you…" Dana continued, moving closer to Suzie to help her sip the cool contents of the glass. "You took everything you could. They found cocaine in your blood—cocaine! How on earth were you able to get this stuff? Why, Suzanne? Aren't the meds working?"

Suzie opened her mouth to reply, then shut it again. What could she say? How could she explain to these normal people that life was too hard, her brain was too far gone? How would they even begin to understand? Hour by hour, sometimes, minute by minute, there were highs and lows and terrible thoughts, there were visions, and doubts, noises, and more and more, the voices.

Like a yo-yo, going up and down, day and night, it never stopped. It never, ever stopped. She had a vague memory of snorting coke with one of the girls from the year above her, but she wasn't sure. She was too wasted… There was whiskey there also and weed, and she knew she'd had a fair amount of those too. Then, there was no memory at all. It just sort of went black—and now she was here, attached to all these tubes, watching her mother fall apart because of her. Even for Suzie, this felt like a spectacular screw-up.

"You're not taking the meds are you?" Robbie said.

This time he was looking directly at her, but he looked weary and troubled. She searched his face for any of the love she thought they shared, but found no trace of it. She felt a sudden swooping sensation in her stomach, fearing maybe this was the moment she'd finally lost him.

"The pills don't work. The psychiatrist doesn't listen to me so I'm better off dealing with this on my own," Suzie said, turning her face to the wall. "They made me fat anyway."

There was a pause while the others took this in. Robbie glanced at Dana. Their faces echoed the sense of helplessness they both felt.

"If you don't take your meds, we'll have to have you committed. Is that what you want?" Dana's voice was harsh now. She was suddenly swamped by anger. The years of worry, the compromises, the appointments, the problems, the fears, had finally left her feeling a rage she felt ashamed to possess.

"If you don't take them, I'll do whatever I have to do to stop you sabotaging your mental health—and your life. This has gone far enough. You only survived this overdose because one of the students panicked and called the ambulance. You could've died..." Dana was trembling now. Robbie put a hand on her shoulder and turned to the troubled young woman who lay watching them, silently, on the hospital bed. Her hands were clenched tight now.

"Suzie, it's time to change. We love you and we can't sit back anymore and watch you hurt yourself like this. We can't do it. Babe, you need to do this."

Suzie looked up at Robbie quizzically.

He doesn't love you. No one could. See how he's plotting with Dana? She's complicit, too. He's betrayed you. Everyone has.

Suzie tried to block out the voices, but weren't they sort-of right? How could he preach to her when he was the one who got her into weed? When he was the one who told her how beautiful she was and made her trust him? He was the only one she believed in— and now he'd just betrayed her, like everyone else.

They didn't understand her. Neither of them wanted her anymore. They wanted to lock her up because she was an embarrassment, and just forget about her. Throw away the key. The voices said all this and more, they went hog-wild on Suzie now. Everyone was against her. They'd conspire with her psych. He'd put her away forever.

"Get out," she said, harshly.

"Suze? Babe? We're trying to help you…" Robbie said, his voice breaking.

"Listen to us, Suzanne, you need to take the medication or I will have you committed, so help me God," Dana repeated.

"Both of you. Get the fuck out now."

Days later, when Suzie was released, after she'd been started on a new course of medication, after she'd promised to keep taking it and agreed this really was her last chance, she returned to her dorm room. Dana's threat to commit her had turned out to be empty anyway. Suzie googled it. She couldn't be committed against her will. She'd have to do far worse than just slap Chloe for that to happen.

But how could she trust her mother now? Or even Robbie for that matter? They wanted to lock her up. Throw her in a cage like an animal. Suzie had read *One Flew Over the Cuckoo's Nest* in high school. She knew what they would have in store for her in an institution. Still, her mom and boyfriend seemed to care about her. They only wanted the best for her, right? Maybe she should listen to them, after all?

But the voices erupted in ferocious disagreement. *Robbie doesn't care about you. It's just an act. They're trying to trick you. What if they lie? Say you really hurt someone this time? No! Take your life into your own hands now. While you still have the chance.*

As Suzie surveyed the room she shared with Andrea, she couldn't help but wonder: would anyone miss her? Would they even notice she'd left?

She pulled her backpack from underneath her bed, and slowly, carefully, as if she were counting the seconds, she folded a sweater, some jeans, a few tops and underwear.

Another text came in from Robbie. *Babe, answer me.*

She looked at it, one of the many he'd sent over the past few hours. She turned off her phone without replying. That went in the backpack too along with her charger, and a notebook. Reaching under her roommate's mattress, she found Andrea's secret bundle of cash, which, it turned out, wasn't that secret. If Suzie felt a pang of guilt, she buried it quickly.

They'll destroy you if you don't go…

Suzie held a bag containing the schizophrenia medication she'd dutifully picked up from the pharmacy, and hesitated.

Would this turn out to be another Ritalin decision?

Then, she turned, dropping the bag of poison to the floor, kicking it under her bed. She picked up her backpack.

Suzie took a deep breath, reminding herself why she had to leave. She couldn't let her mother and Robbie control her. She knew of their deceit, their cunning plots against her. It was only a matter of time before she'd be a prisoner, locked in some sterile institution somewhere with Nurse Ratched no doubt. Without looking back, Suzie shut the door, leaving behind her old life, unsure where to go or who to run to.

Part Two

Moles

Chapter 9: Wonderman

It was the first light of dawn when the Greyhound bus pulled into the station. Suzie was dozing, her head lolling against the window glass.

"Wake up, stranger. Welcome to Vegas." An old, grizzled man, whose missing-toothed grin Suzie didn't immediately recognize, nudged her gently. "This is where our paths part, sugar. Bus don't go any further, so you might wanna try your luck here. Take care of yourself, beautiful."

For a moment, Suzie had no idea where she was. She jolted awake, scanning her surroundings through the window to find neon lights flickering against the fading darkness of the early morning sky.

The man grinned at her as he pulled his bag from the overhead shelf. He looked scruffy, with a bandana tied around his head and a thin cigar in his mouth, whistling as he went. He was vaguely familiar as someone who had been hanging around for a few hours—or was it days? Suzie had a feeling they met in Chicago but couldn't be sure.

Didn't matter anyway. Just another person who darted in and out of her life, just like all the others. Here one minute, and then, gone. Disappeared.

Emerging from the vast, black expanse of the desert, a glittering oasis of civilization appeared, its vibrant energy in stark contrast to the barren landscape. She observed people hustling about, their faces illuminated by the harsh, white glow of the bus station's strip lights.

It must have been early, yet there were loads of cars on the road, people coming and going and a whole bunch of guys who looked like they had nowhere else to go. Suzie knew the look—she'd been living on the streets for months now. She had no idea exactly how long. The days and weeks had blurred into a mish-mash of half-remembered places and people.

Wandering aimlessly around state by state, Suzie knew she was probably lucky to be alive. She'd had weirdos and freaks follow her. She'd had guys try to hustle her for sex. She's had the kindness of strangers who bought her coffee or breakfast, she'd had knives pulled on her in crack dens. It was all mixed together in the melee and chaos of her days since she left Portland, vowing never to return to her mother, or Robbie either. They'd tried to push her into taking the drugs. Robbie, who'd been at her bedside every day after the overdose, told her over and over that she had to go back on the medication.

She had tried to fight him, but his voice was joined by the hospital psych and her mother's. It had just been too much. Not even knowing why, she'd packed up and fled. She hadn't known where she was going. When the money she stole from Andrea ran out, she had to hustle to get by. Veering between homeless shelters and other charities, hot soup from kind volunteers and begging for money, she'd survived, somehow.

Each time she traded her body for a warm bed and a meal, Suzie felt a pang of guilt and shame, but the desperate need for survival quickly silenced her inner turmoil. So what if she'd had to sleep with a few guys to get a bed for the night and a nice meal? Lost in unfamiliar cities, she joined the countless others who managed to get by with little in their pockets, and only their wits—and their desperation—to keep them alive.

People like the bandana guy had come in and out of her life. She'd learned that drifters came and went, took what drugs or food they could, and then they were gone.

The first time she was offered heroin, she hesitated. The acrid smell of burnt spoons lingered in the air, and she'd seen the hollow-eyed faces of those who had surrendered to its grip. But with the biting cold gnawing at her bones and the gnawing hunger clawing at her stomach, Suzie's fractured and disoriented mind could no longer resist the siren call of oblivion. She only wanted the relief it promised. And the first few times, it gave her that feeling of softness, of exhalation, of numbness to the cold and dirt, the hucksters and pimps.

She drew the smoke into her lungs, sitting on the floor of some squalid room somewhere in Chicago probably, though she couldn't be sure. The effect was instant. As the smoke coiled in her lungs, the drug hit the sweet spot between getting her high and calming her down. That night, she slept where she was, curled up on a filthy sofa, oblivious to everyone, knowing that, finally, she'd found home.

That illusion of comfort had disappeared quickly. Soon, she wanted more. And more. Before long, she was sleeping with anyone who could give her the fix she craved, as she kept on traveling, no money to her name, no end destination in sight, just drifting like all the others.

She'd taken cocaine because it stopped the buzzing in her head, temporarily. She had also smoked weed because it dampened down the voices a little, and yet, these days, it didn't. The voices had gradually become stronger and louder over time. Suzie had traveled across countless state lines, unsure where to go, buffeted by the voices and all the people she encountered along the way.

There was no certainty, no safety to be found anywhere—until now, perhaps. Maybe Vegas could offer her a home, a job. Perhaps this could be a fresh start, a new beginning, a chance to live a life though every day was a struggle, every hour a battle with her own mind.

Suzie heaved her worn backpack from beneath her seat, its frayed straps cutting into her fingers as she hoisted it onto her shoulder. She rose unsteadily to her feet, the bus's stale air clinging to her skin, and joined the hobble of weary passengers stepping into the cool embrace of the night.

She'd traveled part of the way by train with another girl whose name she couldn't recall even now, only hours later. They smuggled themselves by hiding in the onboard restrooms. After they'd shuffled off the train, managing to avoid the ticket inspector, giggling as they staggered into the night air, Suzie followed everyone else, making their way to the bus, where she managed to pay for a ticket from the money she'd earned begging. The bandana guy on the bus had struck her as odd, talking to her as if she was his girlfriend, but he hadn't stolen anything from her, a cursory check of her backpack confirmed that.

What would Robbie think of her now? Suzie couldn't help but ask herself this question. He'd been her rock, if only for a few months. Leaving him had been unthinkable, until it wasn't.

Did he miss her?

Suzie admonished herself for thinking about him. He'd sided with Dana, and broke her trust—and her heart—in so doing. She left, and that part of her life was over, wasn't it?

She didn't know if he loved her or not anymore. She didn't know much about anything, except how to dodge all the robbers, tricksters, pimps, and runaways like herself.

Suzie looked down at her hands in her lap. She appeared alien even to herself these days. Her skin was dry and gray-looking. Her hair hadn't been brushed for months. Her clothes, not washed for a while now, were stiff and greasy. But, she'd survived, and that meant something, right? Suzie Schizo. Living on the streets and still alive to tell the tale. Not a great existence, but it must mean *something* that she was still here.

"So, what are you gonna do now that you've reached the city of lights, young lady?" The man who checked her ticket, smiled over at her.

She shrugged. "Find a job. Find a home. Sort myself out, I guess," Suzie offered.

The man made a whistling noise through his teeth. "Well, I guess you won't be the only one. I hope you find what you're looking for, miss."

The man was gone as quickly as he appeared, leaving Suzie clutching a sleeping bag given to her by a social worker somewhere she couldn't remember. She stepped onto the sidewalk. Around her, people bustled by, their shouts and laughter filling the air, as they searched for loved ones, chattered on their phones, and stumbled in sky-high heels. The mingling scents of sweet perfume and greasy fast food hung heavy in the night air.

"Man, is this for real?" she said as she walked toward the main boulevard that dissected the city. The Strip. Neon-soaked, flashing, pulsating, the hotels and casinos loomed ahead as Suzie walked up from the southern end.

Suddenly, there was noise, music, and the lights. She couldn't find the words to make sense of it all. Half-dreaming, half-frightened by the sudden change in tempo from the bus to the street, she gazed around, looking for something to anchor on to, something to move toward, but there was nothing. She started biting at her nail.

Suzie wandered further up the strip, the boulevard lined with impossibly tall buildings, glimmering hotels, and flashy casinos. The sign for Caesar's Palace shone orange. Further along on the other side of the street, a faux Eiffel Tower stood outside Paris Las Vegas Hotel and Casino, light cascading down each side.

But for Suzie, the ultimate spectacle was the water fountain show outside the Bellagio. Though tired, she was not about to turn down a free show, something to take her mind off her situation for a bit. The artificial lake in front of the Bellagio came alive, with dazzling white lights, and streams of water that danced and shot impossibly high into the air. This particular show was synchronized to "God Bless the U.S.A." the soaring patriotic tune by country-music star Lee Greenwood. Sure, America's great, Suzie thought, except for people like her.

Once the show finally ended, Suzie wandered aimlessly, now conscious of her bedraggled appearance. She hadn't been taking care of herself like she should. Her clothes were tattered and worn. Her face was devoid of make-up, but no one seemed to pay any attention to her, and she found she liked this feeling. No one looked her up and down as if she were trash like they did in other cities. No one looked away when they saw her gaunt face. Here she wasn't noticed at all, and it felt good.

As the minutes, or maybe even hours, slipped away in this clock-devoid city of dazzling lights and constant buzz, Suzie's exhaustion began to settle in, a heavy weight pressing down on her shoulders. Her throat felt parched, her legs wobbled beneath her, and she knew she couldn't keep going much longer. She needed to find somewhere to stay, or to hide away as unobtrusively as she could.

She soon found people like her weren't so welcome on the Strip. The mega-corporations that owned all these flashy buildings had their ways of discouraging transients. So she was eventually forced to veer off the Strip, in time finding herself outside a rundown casino, one that only the locals frequented for its better odds. Suzie decided to walk in.

The place was packed. There were people everywhere; sitting at slot machines, feeding in their cash, people leaning over tables as dice were rolled, cards laid expertly for baccarat. It was a whole new world to her. But as Suzie walked through the lines of flashing slot machines, she was unaware that someone was watching her.

Suzie leaned against the dimly lit bar, the faint scent of stale beer and cigarette smoke hanging in the air. She fumbled around in her pocket, but before she could locate any money, a nearby voice caught her attention.

"Don't worry, I've got this. What'll you have?" The deep, soothing voice emanated from a man seated several stools away. Suzie's eyelids felt heavy, and she struggled to focus on him, rubbing her eyes to clear her vision. The overwhelming brightness of the lights disoriented her, the faces of passersby appearing to leer menacingly.

From the corner of her eye, she could see the two schoolgirls in their little dresses, grinning mischievously from the side of the bar. She knew they were not there, but did that mean any of this was real?

The man leaned against the bar, mirroring Suzie's posture, and dipped his Fedora hat. "You look like you need a drink… My name's Wonderman. That's what folks around here call me anyway," he said as he slid off his bar stool and took the seat next to Suzie, a smile playing on his lips.

Suzie furrowed her brow, trying to make sense of her surroundings as the cacophony of slot machines filled her ears, making it hard to concentrate. As her vision blurred and the edges of consciousness threatened to fade, she heard his voice once more. It seemed distant, as if coming from a far-off place.

She looked around and saw the man, who was probably in his forties. He exuded a rugged charm, his tanned and weathered face framed by a mop of salt-and-pepper hair, and his well-worn leather jacket and faded jeans giving him an air of nonchalant confidence. He grinned once more.

Suzie smiled back though she was unsure. Many men had tried to buy her a drink, and many had then tried to sleep with her or lure her away somewhere. Sometimes, she'd go with them if they offered drugs or shelter, using cheap alcohol or whatever narcotics they supplied to take her mind away from what came next.

Now and then, she had flashbacks, moments during those times when she would startle awake and find a guy on top of her, or two guys trying to make out with her. She'd grab her things and run, preferring the risk of walking alone through the night to whatever might await in their shabby, run-down apartments.

The world was a scary place. This she had discovered. It was a far cry from the side of Portland she'd once lived on. If she ever thought of her mom or her boyfriend, she'd shut those thoughts down as quickly as possible with drinks or drugs. It was best that way. She could not go back. She'd burned those bridges and she had to face life on her own. After all, that was what she'd wanted, wasn't it? As these thoughts crossed her mind, Wonderman spoke up.

"Listen, I know you'll be thinkin' I'm just one of the creeps who pounces on a lady like you wherever you go. You're a beautiful woman, so I don't blame them, but I just wanna know you're okay. Have ya got anywhere to stay?"

He turned to the bartender and, with a small hand gesture, waved him over. Wonderman was clearly known here and that reassured Suzie a little.

"I'm Suzie, and I'll have a beer, thank you," she replied, eventually. The bartender slid her the drink and she gulped it down as fast as she could. It was the first thing that had passed her lips for at least twelve hours.

Wonderman watched her with an amused smile. "Guess you needed that," he said, waving again.

Another beer slid down the bar, and this time he raised his bottle and gestured for her to clink it with hers.

"Cheers. Welcome to Vegas," he said, extending his hand for Suzie to shake.

With the comforting warmth of another beer coursing through her veins, Suzie found herself relaxing in Wonderman's presence. The hunger gnawing at her insides, she didn't hesitate to accept his offer of dinner. The mention of food reminded her she hadn't eaten in a while. The voices had settled, and she began to relax. Wonderman's eyes twinkled with amusement as he observed Suzie hungrily devour her burger in record time. As he ordered her a second, he asked:

"So, y'got anywhere to stay?"

Suzie shook her head, still chewing. She didn't look up. She had no idea she was this hungry. She was past caring about this man's motives.

"Then, you've met the right guy. Come and meet my friends. It's a special place we got, I promise you."

Suzie looked at him, attempting to measure him up. Wonderman was attractive in a worldly way. His eyes were startling blue on his tanned, lined face. It wasn't an unappealing face that looked back at her.

She swallowed, wiped her mouth on a paper napkin. Suddenly, Suzie felt tired. Desperation clawed at her, urging her to trust this enigmatic stranger. In the sea of uncertainty that was her life, right now he seemed like a lifeline, her only hope of finding some semblance of safety. Perhaps they would let her take a quick nap on a booth in here so she could get herself together? The harsh truth was she had nowhere to stay, and this man was offering something. That had to be better than nothing, right?

"Okay, so who are your friends?" she said, pushing away her plate now.

"We call ourselves the Mole People, and, if you let me, I'll show you why…"

Chapter 10: The Mole People

A motley group of people, dressed in tattered clothes and adorned with piercings and tattoos, eyed Suzie suspiciously as they loitered outside the entrance to a grimy, dark flood channel. Wonderman and Suzie carefully navigated their way down the steep, graffiti-covered concrete sides.

The intense sunlight, reflecting off the tunnel's entrance, reminded her of the residual lights from the bars, hotels and casinos flashing only a stone's throw away. But this place was a stark contrast to the world she had just left behind.

Suzie couldn't help but feel a growing unease. Under the unforgiving desert sun, she noticed a sea of discarded bottles, wrappers, and debris strewn across the cracked concrete floor, while a few braziers flickered nearby. There was graffiti everywhere, tags scrawled by residents, odd figures and leering faces that made the place look even more sinister, if that was possible.

Suzie instinctively turned to leave, but Wonderman firmly grasped her arm, his grip leaving no room for argument. A shiver ran down her spine as she wondered what she was getting herself into. He winked at her and smiled.

"It sure ain't the Hilton but it's home, and there's a bed here for you…"

Suzie nodded hesitantly, turning back to face the tunnel, her heart pounding in her chest as a mix of fear and curiosity gripped her.

People moved about, their eyes darting around nervously. They huddled around the fires despite the warm morning. Laughter erupted unexpectedly, mingling with the sharp sting of curses and swearing that filled the air. It sounded like a fight might be about to break out a bit further down inside the tunnel, but it was too dark for Suzie to see that far inside. Noises echoed and distorted. Her exhausted mind struggled to process the surreal scene, causing her to question whether this strange new world was simply a figment of her imagination.

The beer Wonderman bought had settled her nerves, drowned out the rampaging voices that were beating against her brain inside the bar, but now she wondered what would happen next. Desperate for rest, Suzie couldn't help but feel a sense of resentment toward Wonderman for bringing her to this place, introducing her to an odd group of strangers when all she craved was the comfort of a bed and the solace of sleep.

"Long time no see, Wonderman," whispered a man nearby, his voice laced with a hint of sarcasm. He had tied his shirt around his waist. Suzie noticed the man's tattoos, which appeared to dance off his body, their black and green shapes gyrating in the air.

"Yeah, I know," Wonderman murmured back. Many others turned to him as they walked to the entrance, though no one said a word to Suzie, except for a couple of women who eyed her with a mix of curiosity and suspicion.

They headed toward a small group, the faces blurring as the light intensified.

"This is Suzie. She's from Portland but she washed up here with us so we gotta make her welcome."

Was Suzie hearing straight? His tone sounded like this was more a command than a suggestion.

The faces turned to her, each one reacting differently. A woman with dreadlocks that hung down her back narrowed her eyes, scrutinizing Suzie carefully. The blonde woman offered a warm, reassuring smile, while the Black guy gave a solemn nod, his gaze lingering on Suzie for a moment before looking away.

No one said a word. Wonderman didn't seem to mind. He continued: "Consider her one of us now, one of the Mole People…"

Even though she was close to hallucinating, Suzie understood that Wonderman was king of this strange domain. She saw the others shrug and the blonde woman say a brief 'hi.'

Glancing around her surroundings, Suzie realized she was standing at the mouth of a flood tunnel. She'd heard of these tunnels before, seen them on the news maybe? Didn't people get killed or washed away inside them? Didn't they have flash floods or something here in Vegas? It was hard to imagine now, the late summer heat of the desert hanging heavy on the air.

"Mole People?" she said. That phrase leapt out. She wasn't sure she liked the sound of it. Weren't moles blind? Didn't they live in the darkness, preferring life underground, away from the sunlight?

As everyone grinned in unison, Suzie couldn't shake the feeling like they were all in on some joke. The thin woman with brunette hair in dreads, piercings in her nose and lips, and wearing a tight-fitting ripped top, began to speak. Her voice was surprisingly strong for a woman so slight, so strange.

"Welcome to our home, Suzie. I am Lady, Queen of the Apostles, and we're Mole People for sure. These tunnels are where we live 'cause we don't got nowhere else. So, we embrace it. We call this place home, and we're welcoming you into it…"

Was Suzie paranoid or did this self-proclaimed Lady of the Apostles sound like she might be threatening her, in a vague way perhaps, but the feeling was there?

Suzie tried to smile but the beer had made her woozy, the lights were still there in her mind if she shut her eyes, and all she wanted now was the oblivion of sleep.

"She looks tired," said the blonde woman. "By the way, I'm Judy and this here is Jazz, my man. We live here too, and if there's anything we can help you with, you just shout, honey."

Suzie looked over at this woman with gratitude, her shoulders relaxing slightly as she felt a small sense of relief in the midst of her uncertainty. Judy had a kind voice, a sweet face, though it appeared ravaged by rough living. Her hair was once bleached blonde, but now the roots had long since grown through. Her face was puffy but she'd put some make up on, and with it, the impression that she was trying to appear 'normal.'

Jazz, on the other hand, was a skinny Black guy. When he put a hand around Judy's waist, Suzie was startled to see that three fingers were missing. Jazz caught her glance, and said softly:

"Oh we all have a story down here, Suzie. You just don't end up here without one. Lost these three to a man with a machete when I was livin' on the streets of Detroit. Found my way down here after they let me outta the hospital, and here I am to this day."

Suzie blinked. "How long have you been here?" she asked, already incredulous. Wasn't this place supposed to be temporary? Surely, no one would choose to *stay* here?

Jazz smiled but there was sadness behind his eyes, Suzie saw that immediately.

"For longer than I care to remember, Suzie, that's for sure. It's been a few years now…"

Judy turned to him and kissed his cheek. Suzie could feel the love radiating between this couple. She was momentarily comforted, though she didn't know why.

Despite this, all in all, it was definitely a depressing scene. Wonderman seemed to sense Suzie's discomfort. Again, he took her arm, and with a strong grip, led her now into the mouth of one of the tunnels. There was still more graffiti scrawled all across the walls. There were discarded polystyrene cups, cans of cheap beer, and cigarette butts strewn on the floor.

"This here is our tunnel, and your new home, Suzie. You look like you're needin' some shut eye now, and I've got just the spot for you. You'll be close by me, so you won't get hassled during the night. Folks will keep away if they know you've got my protection."

Suzie smiled dully, but inside, she was panicking. Where was he leading her? How did she know he wouldn't attack her? Suddenly, Suzie felt an overwhelming urge to bolt away from here. She looked around warily, but Wonderman had her by the hand, and was leading her firmly into the black of the tunnel. She wanted to cry out but found her throat was dry, her voice frozen by sudden fear.

"Don't worry, baby girl, it'll all be okay. You just need to get yourself a night's sleep and it'll all look different in the morning…"

Suzie swallowed hard. Still, no words came as they proceeded further into the blackness. The tunnel smelled musty and damp. Wonderman was holding a flashlight in his free hand, its light picking up the walls, the concrete floor, the piles of clothing, the edges of peoples' living spaces, as they walked onward. Suzie saw a bicycle, suddenly illuminated, then cast into darkness. Likewise, a small stove, the sheets from a bed, the detritus of people who called this place home.

Suzie started when she realized that Lady, Queen of the Apostles had joined them, silently walking beside Suzie on the other side. If Suzie wasn't about ready to drop, she might have had a chance at running, but exhaustion overwhelmed her now, so much so that she wasn't really sure she even cared what was happening. Her life was surreal already, and this felt like more of the same really. She stumbled and this time, Lady took her by the arm, speaking now with a voice that carried, a voice with authority, though over whom? Suzie wondered.

They reached a part of the tunnel that felt a long way inside, but it was probably less than fifty yards inside the entrance. There was a purple curtain hanging down, the flashlight picked it out as Wonderman pulled it aside. Suzie caught sight of a bed, a clothes rack with a few items hanging on it, a small cupboard with a stack of paper cups and various items: a razor, a small mirror, a pack of cigarettes. There was another curtain at the end. Wonderman opened it, gestured for Suzie to follow him.

Lady was behind her now. Was she there to block any attempt at escape? If so, she was wasting her time, Suzie thought. She was so tired, she'd sleep anywhere, even on a dirty-looking mattress on the floor of this bizarre place, which was the very thing Wonderman was now pointing at. On the other side of the curtain was where he said Suzie should sleep. He dragged in a sleeping bag and nodded at Lady.

"You'll get a good night's sleep here," he said reassuringly, "Lady, why don't y'make Suzie feel at home, make sure she's okay. If y'need anything in the night, just holler."

"If the Lord don't provide, then Wonderman will, you can be sure of that, baby girl," Lady said.

Wonderman was still by the curtain, beckoning her to come through, when Suzie said: "But how will I know what time it is?"

"You don't need to worry about that. You're in Vegas, time don't mean nothin' here," Wonderman replied. Again, he smiled, though the effect was more a grimace in the harsh flashlight.

"Is it safe? What happens when it rains?" Suzie asked, yawning.

"We don't fit into the world up there," Lady explained dreamily, "and sometimes, the world don't think we fit in at all, when it floods so heavy and takes some of us with it. Nature's way of cleaning up once in a while... You'll be fine. There ain't no rain clouds up there today. Get some sleep. You look like you sure-as-hell need it."

Suzie looked down at the mattress, and the sleeping bag now laid out for her as the two walked away a bit, the light bobbing as they went.

The flashlight flicked into the space next to Suzie, where she heard Wonderman and Lady muttering, though nothing she could make out. Suzie decided she was too tired to care. Pulling the damp sleeping bag over her body, she was grateful she couldn't see the condition of the mattress, or the walls, or floors.

Sleep overcame her almost instantly, dragging her from darkness into darkness, back into another fitful dream state where reality and imagination collided and merged.

Chapter 11: Secrets

It was pitch black. Water dripped from somewhere.

Drip. Drip.

There were muffled noises.

Suzie rubbed her eyes. She didn't know where she was. She didn't know how long she'd been asleep. Her chest tightened, and her breaths came in short gasps. As memories of the previous night trickled back like each drip of water, her body gradually relaxed, and her breathing steadied.

Throughout the night, her sleep had been sporadic. She kept waking up, unsure of her surroundings, only to drift back into unconsciousness moments later. The energy from the last Ritalin pill she took on the Greyhound had long since worn off and she felt agitated, shaky. There were noises close by: people yelling, people sniffing and laughing, rustling, then the flare of a match and the smell of heroin being cooked up.

Disoriented, she would sit up on her elbows, wait, though she didn't know for what, and then sink back, back into sleep, pulled into oblivion, until the next episode. At times, she wondered if her mind had finally collapsed in on itself, and this was the end.

Confused and still exhausted, Suzie saw a narrow beam from a flashlight. She blinked and squinted her eyes as it blazed briefly into her face.

"You're awake," the female voice said.

Suzie had a vague memory of the woman it belonged to. Wasn't she the one who called herself Queen of the Apostles? What did that even mean?

Suzie attempted to sit up but she felt sore from her night on the thin mattress.

"Don't get up, baby girl. Here's a coffee. I've taken the liberty of putting a couple a spoons of sugar in. I always do that when I need a boost." Lady crouched by Suzie's side, looked down at the young woman.

Even though Suzie had clearly lived rough for months—it was obvious in the unwashed clothing she was wearing, the way those clothes hung off her tiny frame, the smell of the road on her—Lady could see she was a beauty.

Her eyes were startlingly blue, her hair jet black, though it looked like it hadn't been brushed in a long time. She had the air of someone unaccustomed to struggle or filth. *She must be from a well-off family; a mom with a fancy house, a dad with a shiny car,* Lady thought, watching Suzie as she sipped the hot drink gratefully.

Lady smiled as she wondered if any of this could be useful. From what Wonderman told her, Suzie had somehow stumbled on Vegas, traveling all the way from Portland, a distance of perhaps a thousand miles or more. What made her leave all that behind? What did she think she would find here?

Lady was puzzled, intrigued. It's not often someone like Suzie washed up here. Usually, it was the regular drunks, pimps, thieves, addicts, and lost souls who the moles encountered.

"Good. When you're ready, I'll show you around. You can meet the folks here again and start getting to know your new family..." Lady smiled, all the while her brain was whirring, calculating what, if anything, Suzie's appearance might foretell.

Suzie smiled. She was starting to feel human again. It had been a long time since she slept anywhere for longer than a few hours. Usually she just allowed herself a quick doze, better to be on alert in case she was robbed, or worse.

She stretched and yawned, pondering how she'd gotten herself this new place, this bizarre haven for all those who had no place above ground, where the slot machines flashed and the casinos loomed on and on along the Las Vegas Strip, never closing, never revealing the time.

Up there, moles were always on the run from something or other, always forced by the topsiders to move on to someplace else. At least here in the tunnels there was some kind of permanence.

As morning approached, Suzie sipped the scalding coffee, wondering what the day would bring. She pulled her backpack over to check if everything was still there, though her brain had begun to feel especially fuzzy and incoherent today. She yawned again, realized there was nothing missing, and got changed into her spare jeans and t-shirt.

The light of the day seemed too bright, too harsh for Suzie as she walked toward the outside, stumbling through the darkness with only Lady's flashlight beam to guide her. Emerging from the tunnel, Suzie blinked and shielded her eyes from the sun's glare. Overwhelmed by the sudden heat, she noticed Wonderman looking up from the joint he was rolling. He nodded to Lady before approaching Suzie.

"Hey, baby girl. How did ya sleep? You look a lot better than ya did last night. Some of these folks are going into town to look for food. The local dumpsters are very generous," he said, grinning. "Why don't ya go with them. You sure look like ya need a good feed, baby girl…"

Suzie hadn't noticed it before, but Wonderman had a single gold tooth on the front side of his mouth. It glinted in the sunshine, lending him a dangerous, even sinister appearance.

"What's the matter, girl, you look like you seen a ghost!" Lady took hold of her arm and drew her to the group where Judy and Jazz were standing by the lit brazier, with some other people Suzie didn't know. She tried to muster a weak smile as they acknowledged her approach. The couple exchanged a tense glance as she approached them, their expressions hinting at an unspoken disagreement or concern that Suzie couldn't quite decipher. Lady sauntered off, a strange smile on her face.

"Are you okay, Suzie? Did you get some sleep?" Judy paused, looked over her shoulder at Lady who turned around as she walked away, using two fingers to push up an imaginary cowboy hat.

"Did they treat you good, honey?" Judy was scanning Suzie's face. She had her arm around the young woman now and was leading her over to Jazz. There was something maternal about Judy, though she was probably only ten years older, but it was hard to tell.

Suzie was finding things hard to follow, and she could also see the ravages of intermittent sleep on everyone else she'd met so far. It aged people, Suzie thought. For a brief moment, she wondered what she looked like herself, whether she had aged too, but that thought vanished as the voices began their usual tirade, and her thoughts become entangled.

The two omnipresent schoolgirls were standing by the brazier too of course, making faces and sticking their tongues out as usual. They looked ever incongruous against this concrete wasteland, with the drunks and homeless who gathered here because they had nowhere else to go.

"Are you okay, Suzie?" Judy glanced at Jazz.

"Baby, why don't you take Suzie somewhere and get a coffee," Jazz said. "I've got some cash from busking yesterday. There ain't nothin' more a crowd loves than a musician with missing fingers. They were generous, so here, take thirty bucks and get yourselves breakfast somewhere nice. I'll go with the others to try to find some food," he added, giving Suzie a wink and kissing Judy on the cheek.

Already, somehow Suzie felt safer with these two around. She had thoughts of escaping last night, but by the time she'd crawled out of her hole, she wasn't sure where else she could go. She's been running for a long time, and she was bone-tired. It seemed like maybe she'd begun to awaken from a bad dream, except perhaps, the nightmare continued. It was too early to say for sure. Even a filthy mattress, in a pitch-black tunnel that existed to stop flash floods from sweeping across this desert city, was better right now than nothing at all. She decided she had run far enough—for now.

"Let's get you cleaned up first, honey. Come to our little place and you can borrow some clothes of mine until you can get yours washed." Judy smiled, and, together, they entered the tunnel, forking into a left chamber rather than straight ahead to Wonderman's lair, and Suzie's strange new home.

The light died out almost instantly. The smell of must and mold was back. They passed others sitting against the wall, chatting or smoking together. One guy appeared to be trying to fix a broken bike, which Suzie found strangely heartening. People here were trying to live, not just survive, and she thought that must take real guts to try and move forward when you had nothing at all, and no opportunities on the horizon.

Judy's flashlight picked out piles of things, obviously sorted and stored as carefully as possible, next to beds with sleeping bags and other small possessions. Suzie squinted at the moth-eaten sofa, only discerning the figures sitting there as she and Judy drew closer. There was a man and a woman, or at least,

Suzie thought she was a woman. It was hard to tell from just the beam of the flashlight.

Judy flicked the flashlight up to avoid blinding them with the beam, and stopped when they approached.

"This here's Debbie and her man Steve. They've lived here for quite a while now, haven't you both?"

The woman (Suzie could tell she was female now, though she was emaciated and haggard-looking, with a scraggly ponytail tied up behind her head), nodded and flashed a wide smile, revealing a mouth of rotten teeth, some missing completely.

"Been here three years now, Judy, though it feels longer, don't it, Steve?" she laughed. Suzie couldn't tell if her mirth was genuine.

She looked to the man sitting beside her. He had a small box open on his lap, and appeared to be in the process of rolling joints. There was a strong odor of weed, and another smell, one Suzie knew well now. It was the odor of burnt plastic or rubber. She looked closer to see the tell-tale signs, and wasn't surprised to see blisters on Steve's fingers, and on both their lips.

"Well, ain't that right," drawled the man, who looked up briefly, then dropped his head again to continue making what was presumably a joint.

Suzie felt a sudden lurch in her belly as she realized she hadn't taken anything for hours now. During her time on the road, she'd tried pretty much everything, from cocaine, to weed, to benzos and crack. The familiar smell of the crack being smoked, the burning plastic stench, brought her back to the cravings growing inside her.

She wouldn't say she was addicted, but her body needed something to take the edge off, to dull the voices and the pain she carried inside. She knew the shock of crack's instant hit, the soaring high, the crashing low afterward.

"Who's this now?" Debbie said, looking directly at Suzie. As she spoke, she fidgeted and jerked her emaciated body. She was wearing a grubby pink vest top and a pair of jean shorts. Her pale legs looked like sticks poking out from them. It was clear even to Suzie, who had never met someone so clearly possessed by drug addiction before, that this woman was using, and it had robbed her of any beauty she may have once had. Her hair was thin and hung lank and limp in the pony tail she'd scraped it back in.

"This here's our newest resident, Suzie," Judy said, "and I'm just gonna give her a spruce-up. She's traveled a long way, I'm guessing…"

Suzie attempted a smile. She wished she could move away with Judy. The sight of Debbie and Steve, and their obvious drug paraphernalia, was making her feel twitchy and unsettled. Darkness enveloped them as they'd ventured deeper into the tunnel, making Suzie feel increasingly claustrophobic, trapped.

"Hi," she muttered, glancing over at Judy, hoping the woman would sense how she felt. Judy looked back at her, and seemed to notice Suzie's discomfort, because she quickly said: "Alrighty, we'll see you guys around. Take care of yourselves. Come on, missy, let's see what we can find for you to wear."

Suzie heard Judy speak as if for the first time. It was a lovely voice, melodious and strong, or it would have been if Judy didn't cough so frequently.

"It's not the cleanest air down here," she shrugged, attempting to explain it away.

"What do people do in here all day? Why would they want to be inside when it's so dark and, and…?" Suzie couldn't find an appropriate word. She could see that this was a place people were scratching out a living. For them, this was home. She didn't want to offend her new friend, and so her voice trailed off.

She was aware that the two schoolgirls were walking behind her. She could hear their footsteps just as if they were walking back from school all those years ago. Suzie was doing her best to ignore them. There was another voice in her head today. She thought it was a new one; a man's voice and it was fatherly, but in a stern, critical kind of way.

Don't trust anyone, they just want your stash… he said, clearly.

Suzie was trying to listen to Judy as they walked on, deeper into the tunnel, but his voice grew louder.

They don't like you, they just want what they can get from you…

His voice seemed to feed off Suzie's vulnerability, growing more insistent with each passing moment. She felt the weight of its presence, like a heavy fog clouding her thoughts and making it hard to concentrate on what Judy was saying.

Suzie shook her head, trying to push him out. Judy walked in front of her and so didn't notice. She kept talking as they went.

"Well, honey, people are mostly escaping something, or they don't got nowhere else to go. It's sad but it's sure-as-hell true. They spend their time trying to block it out or get back on their feet. There's two types of person down here: The ones you know will never make it out, and the ones who just might…"

Suzie noticed the faint scent of burnt candles mixed with the lingering aroma of stale cigarette smoke as they approached Judy and Jazz's makeshift home. A dim, flickering light cast eerie shadows on the tunnel walls. Judy stopped and pointed her flashlight to a bed flanked on one side by a clothes rack hung with colorful clothing. Something that looked suspiciously like a feather boa had been flung over it, and there was a sequined jacket that picked out the flashlight beam, fracturing it into a thousand pieces.

"Which one am I?" Suzie asked, biting her lip. Seeing the way Judy and Jazz had tried to make their space into a small apartment, as if they were living there by choice, Suzie felt suddenly overwhelmed, and frightened. What if she was one of the people that never make it out, and this was it forever?

Judy let out a gregarious laugh. "Oh, from the moment I saw you, I thought 'here's a girl who won't be here for long'." As she said this, she patted Suzie's hand, and she wondered if Judy was just placating her, like she might do with a child.

"So, what happened to you?" Suzie asked as Judy drew a curtain along the other side, rigged up who-knows-how. As Judy rummaged through her clothes, the rustle of fabric and the clinking of hangers filled the small space. Suzie could feel the rough texture of the worn-out leggings and sweatshirt that Judy handed her.

"You need some meat on your bones, baby, but these should be okay," Judy said in response, ignoring Suzie's question. "Take off your jeans and swap them for these leggings. There's a sweatshirt there and a vest top. You'll feel better when you're changed. It's not easy getting used to life down here…"

"How come you ended up living here with Jazz?" Suzie asked, hoping to elicit a response by rephrasing her question.

"Honey, there's a washbowl there and a flannel. It's the best I can do so just give yourself a wash down." Judy sat down on the bed, grasping a towel. She let out a deep breath, looking down at her bed. "My story's the same as many down here. It was drugs that took it all away. I was actually getting to be famous, honey. I had a recording contract, and I was going to be the next big thing. I was a singer, and a song-writer. Then I found cocaine and champagne. They undid me faster than I knew, and suddenly I was here, with nothing.

"Of course, it didn't happen all at once. I kinda had a lid on it for a while, managed to play sell-out performances, then somehow, I missed a few shows. Then, I missed more shows, and my manager ditched me. I took more and more coke, so much that I blew my record contract, blew it right up my nose. In a couple of years, I'd lost everything I'd worked for since I was a little girl, learning piano and singing at my mama's knee…"

Judy's voice was soft now, and even as Suzie listened and heard about the drugs and the chaos, she thought there was still something of her fame and fortune echoing around Judy even now. The feather boa. The well-kept space. The way she still held herself as if she were about to step out onstage.

"That's so sad," Suzie said, simply.

Judy nodded. "I ended up here, with nowhere else to live. My friends had all gotten fed up with me after my using spiraled out of control. I'd lost my fancy apartment and all my beautiful things, but I sure thought I could rely on my people. I slept on a few couches after it all went bad, but they soon got fed up of me. Couldn't keep myself together, honey." Judy smiled as tears glistened in her eyes.

"When I met Jazz, I was thinking it would be best if I wasn't here on this planet anymore. He changed my mind about that," she finished, picking at a smudge on her shorts. "But, honey, look at me going on when I should be paying you the attention! Take this towel and get yourself dry and clothed."

"I've had feelings like that," Suzie said suddenly. At this, the male voice in her head started to bellow:

Don't trust ANYONE. What the hell are you doing, Suzie Schizo? You're just letting another person in who will screw you over in the end. Remember what Robbie did…Don't ever forget what he did to you…

She managed to ignore it, but she had to concentrate very hard. Judy watched her closely now, as if she sensed what was going on.

"Suzie, are you sure you're okay? What do mean you've had feelings like that?"

"I'm fine, honestly, I'm okay," she stuttered in reply. She wasn't about to spill the beans and make everyone think she was a fucking weirdo.

She's just like all the others. She's trying to control you. She wants you committed. Don't trust her. Don't trust ANYONE.

"I mean that when I was really bad, you know sleeping in crack dens and wondering all night if I was going to die, I thought maybe the best solution was to just end it all. It would stop the…"

"…it would stop the, what, Suzie?' Judy asked quietly.

"Nothing," Suzie said. "It doesn't matter."

Later that week, Suzie found herself heading out with Judy, to rummage through the garbage bins, the search for food never-ending.

Instinctively, she liked this woman, despite the chattering and muttering of the voices, saying strange and unsettling things about her. Suzie wished, not for the first time, they'd just shut up for once.

"Come on, Suzie, let's go."

She noticed Judy never called her 'baby girl'. It was a nickname she despised; it felt like ownership.

"Thanks for calling me by my name," she said as they walked into the sunshine, up above the tunnel into the fumes and light of the world above.

"Whatcha mean, honey? What else would I call you by?" Judy laughed, but she knew what Suzie meant. Wonderman called all the new women 'baby girl'. "He did that to me too," Judy said, unexpectedly. "He called me 'baby girl' for a while, saying I was special. By then, I was hooked on everything and I needed the drugs. Still do…"

Suzie hadn't noticed before. Judy's fidgeting. Her constant sniffing. Her drawn appearance. Now, as she peered closer, it was clear.

"He wanted me for sex, and, in exchange for seeing a few guys, he'd give me whatever I needed. I just wish I didn't need it, Suzie. I wish I was free to sing again. There was no feeling like it."

Suzie watched Judy, hoping she wouldn't cry. Something about Judy's past, the sudden loss of her fame and fortune, unsettled Suzie.

"You'll sing again one day…" she tried to reassure her.

Judy shook her head. "I won't, honey, and I know it, though Jazz tells me all the time I will. You're a good person, like he is." She looked at Suzie with a sad smile. "There are good people in this world still, we just have to keep believing that."

Suzie stared, then it hit her. She knew who Judy was. Judy Seal. Music diva, singer, song writer, nominated to win a Grammy. For a moment, Suzie couldn't speak. She stared at the woman's face, seeing past the drug-ravaged complexion and into the up-and-coming star she once was. Didn't Suzie's mom have tickets to see her once? It was a while ago, but Suzie felt sure suddenly that she'd heard Judy's music playing at home. Jeeez.

As if Judy understood what was playing out in Suzie's mind, she got up abruptly.

"Let's take a walk, see what we're missing," she said.

The Strip loomed off in the distance. In front of them was a billboard proclaiming the next star due to begin their residency at one of the colossal Vegas theaters. Judy stopped and shook her head, refusing to walk on.

"That could've been me, Suzie," she whispered, her voice heavy with regret. "It should've been me."

Suzie was at a loss at how to respond. Her head was pounding now, the sun was too bright, its sharp rays too harsh after days—or was it weeks now?—inside the tunnel. Her throat was dry, coated with the desert dust, and she felt a powerful urge to scurry back into the comforting darkness.

They stood together at the roadside, staring at the huge picture of the star, her hair glossy, her face radiant, the very image of wealth and fame.

Suzie put her hand on Judy's shoulder.

"Let's go. We'll find Jazz. It'll all be ok," she said. Except in her heart, she couldn't shake the feeling that, for Judy at least, it wouldn't ever be.

Chapter 12: Baby Girl

Each night, in the blackness, Suzie's dreams grew more vivid. Her mind looped around on itself, as the weed she now smoked daily, combined with the beer, the occasional snort of coke, all mixed with the madness that churned within her.

Most nights, she dreamed of her father sitting at his piano, his delicate fingers poised to play, but before he struck a key, he turned to her and smiled sadly. Then he winked as if it was just them, just the two of them, together again in his strangely silent inner world, while his hands fashioned magic and beauty out of sound.

As his fingers moved, she imagined she could see the notes floating in the air, though her dream always remained silent now—her father's music was always just out of reach. Often, Suzie woke with a start, tears wet on her cheeks, always unsure where she was at first, always wondering if she had finally died and this black night was, in fact, hell.

It was on a night like this that she felt a pull at her t-shirt. Convinced she was dreaming, she roused a bit but soon feel back into her unconscious state. Then, a hand touched her chest, her thighs, moving across her body in a way that felt all too real. When a man's mouth bore down on hers, she spluttered awake. She couldn't tell who it was, but then he spoke.

"Lie back, beautiful. Don't worry, baby girl, you may even like it…"

Suzie recognized the voice instantly.

"Wonderman? What are you doing? Why are you here?" She wasn't yet convinced this wasn't a terrible nightmare, one which she'd yet to awaken from.

Suzie tried to struggle up away from her mattress, but the man she met only a few days ago was heavy against her now.

He was holding her arm while his other hand searched her body. She tried to wriggle from his grasp but he pinned her down, lying beside her. A bolt of fear like white lightening ran through her instantly, and she was wide awake now, alert, her heart pounding, her fear strangling her.

"Come on," Wonderman breathed into her neck, "we could have fun together…" He moved and his body was now on top of hers. Suzie felt she couldn't breathe. She gasped but nothing was drawn into her lungs. She started to cough, then struggled against him again, but found his grip got tighter, his breathing more insistent.

"No…Get off me…" she managed to say as his hands tried to fumble with the waistband of her jeans. He grunted but kept at it.

"No…Wonderman…get off, get off me…" Suzie began to panic. He wasn't listening to her. She tried to fight him off, but he was strong. Holding down her arm, he tried to kiss her neck, his stubble rough against her skin, the smell of tobacco and cheap whiskey on his lips. Suzie was gasping now, the panic coursing through her. She felt like she was drowning in the darkness, and she heard herself whimper.

"Stop! Stop it! Get away from me!" She found her voice. And just then, there was another person speaking. Someone who stepped toward them, a flashlight switched on, its beam hitting Suzie full in the face, blinding her.

"Get off her, Wonderman," came Lady's voice. Suddenly, the priestess was beside her, next to Suzie's mattress, looking down on them. The flashlight shone now onto Wonderman's face. He pulled his arm away, covering his eyes, giving Suzie the chance to wriggle out from under the man's clutches.

"This ain't your business, Lady," Wonderman said, sharply, but he paused, his weight still heavy on Suzie's leg as she attempted to crawl up off the mattress. Her sleeping bag was in disarray, her body was shaking with fear and… something else, something primal, something like rage.

"Just get away from her," Lady repeated with a drawl. Her voice was surprisingly quiet.

From far off in the tunnel, or so it seemed, someone laughed—then cursed. An object was thrown, an argument was erupting. A strange look passed between Wonderman and Lady, one that was intimate and knowing, and then the man did something surprising. He obeyed Lady's command. Wonderman merely shrugged and slowly withdrew from Suzie's bed. He shook his head as he did so, reached into his pocket, and fumbled for something.

A lighter flared. The delicious smell of his rolled-up cigarette filled Suzie's nostrils. She was confused, trembling, unsure what to do next, but Lady waited until Wonderman had slouched off into the black tunnel, trailing smoke, before she sat down slowly on the makeshift bed. Suzie waited for what was going to come next, her mind whirring, a buzzing sound in her ears.

When Lady spoke, her voice was soft. "Don't worry about him. He'll stay away from you now, baby girl. Just get some sleep if you can, it'll all be fine in the morning."

The fractured beam of the flashlight threw strange shadows on the priestess's face. Suzie was too shocked to reply, but she was flooded with gratitude. She stared back at Lady, wondering how she could possibly 'get some sleep'. Who were these people anyway? Why did Lady protect her from Wonderman's assault? And why was she being told it's all 'fine'? It didn't feel fine. She'd had guys do that before and she knew the typical cost of fighting back: a split lip, or worse.

"Come on, baby girl, he just got carried away but I'm here for you, you know that…"

Lady smiled, but Suzie felt no warmth from her. Lady had an other-worldly aura, as if part of her was always somewhere else. Perhaps it was the drugs that so many took down here. Or maybe she really was some kind of priestess. Whatever she was, there seemed to be a distance between them that felt unbreachable, unknowable, and Suzie couldn't figure out if it was Lady's real nature or some kind of power play.

Whatever it was, Lady seemed unconcerned by what she'd just witnessed. She alighted off the mattress, smiling back at Suzie in a vague kind of way, and slinked off into the dark, the light bouncing off the tunnel walls as she went.

Soon Suzie heard the pull of the curtain that enclosed Wonderman's space, then a low muttering of both male and female voices. Suzie blinked, unable to process what had just happened, but she was sure of one thing—it was time to go.

She looked toward the curtain, every sense in her body jangling, but with exhaustion in there too. As quietly as she could, she got out of the sleeping bag. As she moved, she prayed it was still night, all the better to hide her escape. For once, the voices were silent as she gathered her backpack, the clothes Judy gave her, the few personal possessions she still had.

Satisfied she had everything, she crept through the tunnel, pausing like a frightened mouse at every sound. The darkness enveloped her like a suffocating blanket, yet her instincts guided her toward the exit, the faint scent of gasoline fumes from the busy road nearby that mingled with the damp mustiness of the tunnel.

Taking a deep breath, Suzie cautiously approached the curtained area that defined Wonderman's lair. Her heart pounded as she listened intently for any sign of him stirring, acutely aware of the danger if she got caught. She didn't hear anything, sense anything, and she took this as a good sign, a reason to move onward.

Barely able to breathe, she crept on and on, and then, once she was sure she'd put Wonderman behind her, she was suddenly startled. A flashlight turned on. Suzie was momentarily caught in the brightness of its beam. It was pointed straight at her. She squinted into the darkness, unsure whether to run, unsure what to do. It was Debbie's voice she heard now.

"What'cha doing, Suzie. It *is* Suzie ain't it?" she drawled, grinning at her with her rotting teeth. "Sweetie, if you're trying to escape, then know this: He won't let you go. You're his prize possession now, and he *will* come after you and he'll hunt you like a deer in the forest. Wonderman knows everyone around these parts…"

Suzie swallowed. She couldn't think what to say. Was this a hallucination? The beam of light seemed too strong, too glaring, to be a figment of her mind. Debbie stepped forward. Her face was alarmingly gaunt, her eyes looked troubled, she twitched and shook, but she appeared also to be blocking Suzie's path out of the tunnel to—what? Was there freedom out there, or just another trap waiting for her? Suzie didn't have time to think about it further.

"What do you mean, I'm a prized possession? And who are you talking about?" Suzie said.

Debbie issued a laugh, but again the sound was hollow, completely devoid of any mirth or joy. "Oh, I think you know who I'm talking about, sweetie. Wonderman, of course! He hasn't taken his eyes off you since you washed up here, Little Miss Strange, with your troubles and your big blue eyes. No wonder Lady stopped him. She don't want no girl from out-of-town showing up and knocking her off her perch!

"Oh, don't worry, honey, we all know everything that goes on in these here tunnels! Lady can't bear to see the way he looks at you. Sure, he's been with all of us at some point, but he's never put one of us up on a pedestal with Lady until you —no, she can't have that."

Debbie grinned and the effect was alarming. She looked up and down haltingly, appraising Suzie who was rooted to the spot, wondering what came next.

"Wonderman could make a killing with you," Debbie said. "They'd be lining up around the block for you, opening those pretty little legs of yours and paying good money for it! Why do you think he rules this roost? Because he can and because he'll do anything to keep you.

"He used to look at me that way, and look what happened to me," Debbie croaked as she grabbed Suzie's arm.

Suzie's cry echoed through the tunnel, each passing second intensifying the pain from Debbie's surprisingly strong grip.

"I won't warn you again," Debbie said. "Run off, see if I care, but you'll be looking over your shoulder every last day of your life…"

"Get the hell off me!" Suzie yelled, but as she did so, she heard a chuckling sound behind her.

"Baby girl, we knew you might take flight and soar away from us. I took the precaution of having someone here, day and night, to watch over you. Debbie's right. We want you to stay…" Wonderman grinned. He reached out, stroking Suzie's cheek, making her bristle.

She swiveled around, the full gravity of her situation dawning. She was trapped, just as surely as if someone had turned a key in a lock. She stared back at him, anger building inside her, fear pounding in her body. Behind her, Debbie snorted, as if amused.

"Let's all just get some sleep. It's early still, and baby girl, you look like you need a rest. Let Debbie take you back to your bed. She'll make sure you're nice and settled down…"

"Don't call me, baby girl," Suzie said. "I have a name…"

Wonderman merely smiled, and the effect in the beam of the flashlight wasn't appealing.

When it was clear he didn't intend to respond, Debbie pushed her forward. Wonderman grinned back at them both, apparently satisfied with his night's work. Suzie felt a sharp pang of anger again, the heat of it. She wondered if she could outrun both of them in her current state.

I need to score something… she thought. Her body had begun to shake. Beads of sweat formed on her brow as her instincts became muddled by the overpowering urge. Perhaps she could try to fight her captors? Something told her they would overpower her—and relish the chance. Knowing it would be over before it even began, she glared at Wonderman, who still smiled as she shuffled past, back to her bed in the bowels of the tunnel. Debbie's footsteps echoed behind her.

Wonderman turned, watching her disappear into the dark. He'd had his eye on Suzie ever since she'd appeared in the casino. He couldn't shake his attraction, and it made him soft on her. Any other girl would be working on her back for him by now, in return for his protection, for the drugs he supplied, for a place to sleep in relative safety.

He'd always seen himself as part-savior, part-devil. He knew what he did. He didn't feign modesty or shame. And yet, this girl seemed to have penetrated where many had failed—his heart, such that it was.

He had plans for her. She would be stupid to reject his offer of work, and he'd supply only the highest paying clients, only the guys who were clean and safe, and he knew he'd be watching over that too, making sure they treated her right. In his mind, it all made perfect sense, yet he hadn't been able to do it just yet.

Suzie was special. His head said she'd still have to work for him, that was his right if they wanted his protection, but with her, with her he would do it right, he'd make sure of it, though his heart said different.

Rarely, if ever, did he feel anything more than a twinge of, what? Of guilt, perhaps? Of responsibility? Not even that. He was a survivor, and he lived by the law of the streets: kill or be killed. Become the top dog at any cost, because there was safety that way.

He watched Debbie as she slowly disappeared into the darkness, escorting Suzie back to her bed. "Cheap whore," he muttered, looking at her as she went. The drugs he'd given Debbie over the years had ravaged her, that much was clear. She was just a shadow of her former self now. Debbie was once 'someone.' She was once a star, albeit for a porn studio, but a star nonetheless. Drugs, bad luck, and bad men all combined to send her fleeing, away from those she could never repay.

Wonderman had found her when she was still a stunner, with thick, long brown hair, a figure most guys would kill to get their hands on, and full lips, made fuller with cosmetic adjustments, just like her chest. She was on the run, and he gave her a place to live—and security too, though she'd had to work for it of course. It was only a few short years later, and Debbie was skinny, her figure had disappeared, and her skin was gray and covered in acne. Her price had fallen steadily, while her need for crack had only increased.

She's little use to me now, she's becoming a liability, Wonderman thought as the darkness finally enveloped the women.

Inside Suzie's head, the buzzing had grown and grown until it felt like it might burst. She was trembling now—hard. The tunnel's walls felt like they were entombing her, moving inward to crush her. She finally dropped down onto her mattress, and as she did so, she reached instinctively inside her bag. There was a small blade hidden in a side pocket. She pulled it out, hands shaking, the pressure building and building. When she drew it across her arm, she exhaled audibly. The pain seemed to fade away, while the blood flowed.

Chapter 13: Searching

Dana collapsed onto the worn-out sofa, her weary eyes focusing on the flickering television screen. It had been a long day, calling police stations and hospitals in various states. She still refused to give up hope of finding Suzanne.

The day the university had called, months ago now, to tell her Suzanne was missing, was not one she ever wanted to relive. And yet that conversation—especially on nights like this when she was dead tired, when there was still no news—still churned around her head:

"Mrs. Franks?"

"Yes, can I help you?" Dana said, holding up her cell phone.

She almost didn't answer it; she was in the middle of something at work, but something told her to take the call.

"This is Dr. Fedowski at Hudson University. Is this a good time to speak?"

Dana paused, exhaling quickly. She had to finish these accounts before she could leave that night, and this was just another interruption. Why did it always have to be about Suzanne?

"Yes, of course," she answered, without meaning it.

"I'm sorry to tell you, Mrs. Franks, that Suzanne is missing, and has been for two days now."

For a moment, Dana thought she'd misheard.

"Missing? What do you mean, she's missing? She must just be with a friend, or that young man Robbie she's seeing?"

A tight knot had formed in Dana's throat, making it difficult for her to force out the words.

"No one has seen her, including her roommate Andrea and her boyfriend. Mrs. Franks, she left with some things. Her bag was missing, and so were some of her clothes, and her roommate's money was gone."

"Did she take her medication with her?"

"I'm sorry, Mrs. Franks, I don't believe she'd been taking it for some time. We found a bag filled with her meds under the bed…"

Dana dropped her phone. She sat and stared at her computer screen, the numbers and words suddenly meaningless. Suzanne was missing. She had failed her.

A tidal wave of grief crashed over her, quickly chased by panic and confusion. She was paralyzed with indecision. Who should she call? What should she do? Suzie had left the hospital by herself, not wanting to be taken back to campus by Dana or Robbie.

Dana had been hesitant, but decided to respect Suzie's wishes and give her some space before calling her. Was that the wrong thing to do? Was that just the 'space' Suzie needed to decide to leave, to run away? She couldn't be sure. Maybe she'd met someone else? That seemed impossible in the few days since her discharge. Nothing was certain, except that Suzie had left, without leaving any message behind.

The day had blurred into fits of tears, in between endless phone calls, being asked to wait, to be put on hold, until someone in each department across the city could speak to her. No one had seen Suzanne. She'd vanished into thin air.

From that moment forward, Dana had called every police department and hospital in Oregon. She stopped sleeping. She stopped eating. Every waking moment was consumed with trying to find her. She drove around the city, then further afield, hoping against hope she might see her somewhere. No sign of Suzie.

As the weeks and months progressed, she didn't stop. Dana finally quit her job to keep up the search, her scope widening and widening. But still nothing. Dana still called police departments in multiple states, even though Suzanne's disappearance was old news now. There had been no indication at all that she was still alive—except perhaps one time, but she couldn't be sure. Every day the grief, the anger, the guilt, just grew stronger.

One evening early in the summer, she uncorked a bottle of chilled white wine and filled her glass. With a sigh of relief, she slipped off her heels and tucked her legs beside her on the sofa. Absentmindedly, she flicked through the channels on the TV when a documentary caught her eye.

Dana wasn't particularly interested, but she'd grown to despise the silence that permeated her home, so the background noise that the TV provided was always welcome. She glanced up, her curiosity piqued by the subject matter. Suddenly, her eyes widened in shock. The wine glass slipped from her hand, crashed to the floor and shattered into a hundred jagged pieces.

Chapter 14: Prayers

The light flashed harshly on Suzie's face, a face still wet with tears. She blinked, but otherwise didn't react. Her mind had gone somewhere else, drifting away, out of this place. Lady was here now, smiling and holding a Starbucks coffee.

"Hey, baby girl. How's it going today? I got you this. It's fresh from the coffee shop and I had them put in two shots…"

Suzie forced herself to wake up fully.

"Go on, take it—don't let it get cold. Listen, I got you some nice clothes last night too. One of the girls had some nice things she didn't want anymore. I saved you the best ones. We can go check them out together," Lady added, handing the flashlight to Suzie.

"When you're ready, I'll be waiting. Come with me to my church service. I'll be preaching today, I'd like you to be there, so I'll give you a minute to sip on that coffee and get up."

Suzie looked down at the coffee cup in her hand, the steam rising in the beam of the flashlight. Lady had already walked off, and Suzie wondered what this would portend. Why would a girl just *give away* nice things in here? Were they stolen? Were they taken by force and intended to pacify her? Nothing was certain in this place. People seemed so helpful, but she always expected there'd be a high price to pay for anything she received.

A few minutes later, and Suzie was walking to Wonderman's space, knowing Lady would be waiting for her. When she arrived, she found Wonderman sprawling across his bed, his Fedora perched sideways on his head. He tipped his finger to her, just as she'd seen Lady do, and smiled warmly.

"How did you sleep, baby girl?"

Suzie bit her lip, searching for the words but coming up empty.

Lady was also lying on the bed, close against Wonderman. She got up and gestured for Suzie to follow her.

"So, you guys are together," Suzie said more as a statement, as they moved together through the tunnel.

"You think right, though we're both free spirits…" Lady said in a sing-song kind of way. She took long, bounding strides, which reminded Suzie of the way a gazelle moves. There was an elegance to Lady's gestures and motion, which seemed out of place in this dark underworld. Not for the first time, Suzie wondered how she came to be here.

"How come you live down here in this mole hole?" Suzie said, emboldened by the deadened feeling in her heart, the disconnection she felt growing and growing each moment.

"Oh, baby girl, it's a long story, and I don't share it with many people so why don't you just relax and thank your lucky stars you found us, your new family of Mole People.

"And Suzie, take a word of advice from me. You don't wanna upset Wonderman, honey," she added, stopping and turning to Suzie, staring her full in the face. "And you don't wanna go asking too many questions. Everyone down here has their secrets, we wouldn't be here otherwise."

Lady's eyes were vacant as she stared back at Suzie. It was Suzie who averted her gaze first.

"Oh baby," Lady said, taking hold of Suzie's arm and pulling up the sleeve to reveal more of the fresh cuts, the dried smeared blood, "Wonderman don't like his goods spoiled. You might wanna rethink those cuts, they're not a good look on you…"

Suzie pulled her arm away, covering up quickly, the shame burning inside her. It was not until they reached the second tunnel that Suzie realized what Lady had said. She said she was Wonderman's *goods*. Suzie didn't like the sound of that at all.

There were a few people gathered in the far reaches of the adjacent tunnel, a place just as dark, damp, and grim as the one they'd come from. Lady, Queen of the Apostles, took her place, her chin raised upward, her arms outstretched. Someone lit a candle, and the service began:

"…We're forgotten by everyone, especially those who're up there in the bright lights, drinking and gambling. We don't exist no more…"

Lady cast her gaze around the tunnel for emphasis. There were several people, a disheveled woman wearing a filthy t-shirt. She was holding a small dog which, unlike her, appeared well fed. There were a couple of men, one standing barechested, his rangy, muscled body covered in homemade tattoos; one of a man's face and one of a woman's, marked into his chest. He was twitching and murmuring under his breath, while a cigarette dangled precariously from the corner of his lips. The other man was on his knees, his head bowed, babbling, it seemed, some kind of incoherent prayer.

"They don't know that it's *we* who are the Apostles, the chosen ones. We've all been damned. They don't want us up there. We don't fit. We're not valued. We have no choice but to stay down here, away from the light, in the darkness, to await our ascension…"

With this, Lady raised her arms upward, and closed her eyes. She held like this as the kneeling man shouted 'Amen!'.

It was then that Wonderman pulled Suzie aside.

"I want you to come with me," Wonderman said, slowly, as if she were stupid. She didn't want to go. She yearned to flee, but an irresistible urge gnawed at her, a craving for something, a calling for *something* to take her back out of herself, to absent herself from all of this; from the threats and veiled promises, the people and the despair, the darkness, the filth, and the dank air.

As if Wonderman sensed it too, he pointed his finger and nodded solemnly. They walked back to his curtained lair, where he sat down and patted the bed. She clutched her arms around herself, attempting to keep her guard up. But with every step, she felt the weight of exhaustion bearing down on her. The fight seemed to have drained from her, and though she was still wary of him, she knew what was in store.

There was always a strange intimacy, one that was immediate and absolute, in the moments before scoring drugs or sharing them. Barely any words were expressed. Barely anything was actually spoken. They both knew how this ceaseless ritual of the underworld was performed. They both knew that the drugs would be taken from wherever they'd been concealed, and they would be laid out. It was the timeless beat of the tunnels, the call of drugs, the endless craving about to be satisfied. There was a delicious pause as she waited, knowing Wonderman would produce something, she didn't yet know what.

Wonderman brought out a pouch, she didn't see from where. He reached inside it and drew out a small package of white powder. Suzie knew instantly it was coke. He tipped a small quantity out onto a mirror, and pulled a credit card out from the pocket of his jeans. Suzie could see even by flashlight that the numbers had been rubbed off, and it looked chewed on one end, its financial powers plainly long expired. But it was still useful for something.

Grasping the thin plastic card, he scuffed the powder into two lines. Then, he looked up and, graciously, gestured for Suzie to go first. She pulled her hair back, and leaned over, snorting the powder up into her nose. The effect was immediate.

With a swift jerk of her head, she inhaled sharply to clear her nose. A fantastic buzzing started, not like the usual noise she heard, but a high jangling note that made her feel energized and suddenly focused. Wonderman leaned over and did the same.

He smiled at her, and despite everything she knew about him, Suzie found herself smiling back. It was Lady who broke the spell. Footsteps announced her arrival, and then the curtain was pulled back. She pointed her light first at Wonderman, and then at Suzie, then she smiled too.

"I see you're both getting along just fine now," she said, smirking. "Don't get too cozy, baby girl, he'll make you pay for his hospitality." Lady laughed, but Wonderman scowled.

"Shut your damn mouth," he said. "You always take things too far. Suzie's my business, not yours. She don't have to pay anyone a thing," he said.

"…at least not yet…" Lady added.

Wonderman glared at her, but the strange priestess seemed unperturbed.

Suzie looked anxiously back and forth at them, confused now. She had never seen these two exchange a harsh word, let alone quarrel so bitterly.

Lady narrowed her eyes. She turned to Suzie.

"I know what's going on here. I was trying to protect you, baby girl. I shoulda left you in his clutches. I stopped him that night, don't you ever forget it," she spat regretfully.

"Get outta here, you fucking bitch," Wonderman drawled, though he was now reaching back in his pocket, and Suzie guessed he wanted another hit. She couldn't help herself. Even though she loathed him, the lure of another line was too much. She stayed put, knowing she'd made an enemy of Lady.

"I coulda pimped you out, Suze. I don't know why I don't. I must be getting soft…" Wonderman began, reaching out to caress Suzie's knee.

Instantly, it hit her. She leapt up off the bed, unsure what to do exactly, but somehow knowing she must leave now, despite her craving for more. She yanked the curtain open. Stumbling, she tried to make her way toward the faint light of day.

"Hey, where you going?" Wonderman's voice followed her, but she ignored him. This was it. She had to get out of here. The heat was intense now, and all the other moles seemed to have come inside the tunnel, crouching, sniffing, cursing, yelling, and drinking along the edges. She sprinted past them, past the entrance of the tunnel and into the blinding light outside, but then she stopped.

She must have been hallucinating.

"Suzie? It's you, isn't it? Thank God I've found you…"

Chapter 15: Robbie

Robbie stared back wide-eyed at the ghostly apparition before him, barely able to comprehend that this was the girl he had once adored.

"Suze? Suzie is that you?"

For a moment, Robbie thought he must have been wrong, that he'd driven through the nights in search of his girlfriend for nothing. The woman standing in front of him was almost unrecognizable.

She was skeleton-like. Her once beautiful black hair, that hung so low down her back, and which he liked running his hands through, was now grimy and disheveled. Her creamy pale skin was now a dull lifeless gray, and her once piercing blue eyes appeared clouded and glazed.

Then this terrible spectre of a woman, in a gesture he knew so well, tucked her hair behind her ear and looked down at her feet. In that instant, he was sure it was her.

It fell on Robbie to be the first to discover that Suzie was missing. Her roommate Andrea was gone, back home in California to attend her sister's wedding. For days, Suzie hadn't been replying to any of Robbie's texts, or taking his calls, or even answering her door when he knocked.

Eventually, he went to the dean and expressed his concerns about her. They'd gone into her room that day—to find her backpack and a few possessions missing. Robbie sat heavily on the bed, his face in his hands. "I've failed her, I've fucking failed her."

Since that moment, he'd vowed he would find her. But after weeks and months of following cold leads, of driving around Oregon, of calling hospitals and police departments, eventually he'd given up. When Dana called him to say she'd seen someone in a TV documentary who looked like Suzie, and she was living in a Las Vegas storm tunnel, he didn't hesitate at all.

"Are you sure it was her?" he said. He was in the middle of studying when his cellphone rang and Dana's name had flashed on the screen.

"No, I'm not sure, but it sure as hell looked exactly like her. She was hanging around by those flood channels in Las Vegas, and the camera caught her face square-on. It was a documentary about 'the Mole People,' or that's what I think they're called. Robbie, those tunnels are dangerous, and she looked like she hadn't eaten in weeks…"

Robbie ran his hand through his blond hair. "Alright, I'm jumping in my car and heading down there. I'll call you when I get there."

There was a silence as Dana gathered herself. Eventually, she croaked: "Thank you, Robbie. I can't ever repay you for this, for your kindness…"

"It's nothing. I'm on my way there now," he said and ended the call.

Within minutes, he'd packed a bag and was speeding out of the city in his Mustang, knowing he would be driving all night, just to see if she was, in fact, the girl he'd let down so much.

"Suzie, it *is* you! I knew it! Oh my God, look at you…"

Suzie stood motionless and mute, like a startled rabbit glued to oncoming headlights. Could it really be him? The man who sided with her mother, who betrayed her? Somehow, none of that seemed to matter anymore as she gazed up at him.

"Robbie… is it you? How did you find me?" she said finally, stumbling over her words, blinking in the light and heat as if she truly was a mole. Suzie was momentarily dazed, transported back to their days under the stars, the nights spent together, the whispered promises of undying love. She couldn't believe he was really standing in front of her now, after all she'd been through—after what she'd become.

"I'm so sorry, Robbie… I… I couldn't stay. They were going to lock me up in one of those places, and you were going to help them do it."

"Oh Suze, you have it all wrong. We only wanted to help you—but shit, you look terrible, like really bad. Why didn't you just come back? We coulda worked this out, babe." Robbie stepped back, pulled his hands through his hair as he always did when he was stressed or overwhelmed. Then she saw it: the tilt of his head, the slight curl of his lip. The look of revulsion mixed with shame.

"Suzie," he finally managed, "When your mom saw the documentary about the people who live down here, she couldn't believe it when she saw you. Even though you were in the background, she recognized you. I came here to bring you home, Suzie. You need help…"

Suzie shook her head forcefully, her heart pounding now, her palms sweating. She obviously needed something to take all this away, to take away the shock, the shame, and the pulse of anger stirring within her.

"My mother saw a documentary? Why would she call you anyway? You both cooked this up together, didn't you? Come and rescue poor Suzie, then throw her in a mental asylum! Shit, Robbie. You'd think I'd fall for that?"

She had a vague idea that there were men with cameras a while back, but she couldn't recall the details. There were always people coming and going, even a social worker or two now and then, trying to fix them. Cynicism always greeted them in return, and Suzie guessed she'd picked that up too because all she could now think was that this was a plot to lock her up again.

Her vision started to blur, and she could feel herself trembling. As her cravings intensified, the memory of escape, of coke, consumed her thoughts, making it increasingly difficult for her to focus on the situation with Robbie.

Then she caught sight of Wonderman, still standing nearby, listening. Strangely, he now felt like her only friend. Wonderman merely gestured to his pocket, and she knew he had some more powder for her.

"Suzie?"

Robbie seemed to melt away as the cravings hit her like a strike of lightning.

"Look, I don't know. I need to think. Robbie, I can't come home. They'll take me, and you'll let them. You and Mom'll have me locked up, I know it. I know it…"

Suzie was shaking more and more as this painful exchange continued. Where at first she was thrilled to see Robbie, the man of her heart, now she was wary. The bad thoughts were starting to crowd out her mind.

He's lying to you. He wants to put you in a psych ward. He's going to kidnap you. Don't listen to him, he's just like Mom. He's lying…

She needed a hit now, badly. Her brain felt like it was finally unravelling for good.

Robbie stared back at her, cold, as if he'd never known her. He was at a loss as to what to do. Here was the woman he'd cared for, tumbling downward in a spiral of self-destruction. She wouldn't believe he had her best interests at heart. She was ill, needed help, but she wouldn't let him, and it weighed heavily on his heart. This was his fault. He should have never introduced her to weed.

"I tried…" he began to stammer.

By now, a crowd of onlookers had gathered, their curious eyes reflecting a mix of concern and intrigue. Among them, a middle-aged man with a fedora hat and an air of authority stood out, slouching against the shadowy entrance to the tunnel. He appeared to be observing carefully, gleaning all the information he could about this unwelcome intrusion into what was apparently his domain.

"Can I help you? My name's Wonderman, and I'm one of Suzie's friends here…"

He stared down Robbie baldly, challenging him to do— what? What could Robbie do—without dragging Suzie up the bank, throwing her in his car, and driving like hell back to Oregon?

Robbie clenched his fists. "I don't need your help, and neither does Suzie. This doesn't concern you," he said, raising himself up to his full height. He was an imposing figure too, but he wasn't sure how far to take this, not sure if this shady-looking dude in front of him might be packing a knife or some other weapon.

"I think you'll find Suzie wants my help, don't you, baby girl?" Wonderman cast a glance back to Suzie, but remained where he was, staring down Robbie.

Suzie nodded but dropped her gaze to her feet. If only she could have some time to process all of this. Robbie's appearance was a shock; she could really use something to take the edge off it. She was fidgeting now, rubbing at her nose. She finally looked up and caught the look on Robbie's face. It seemed almost one of disgust. She saw clearly that he was sickened by her, by her appearance, yet still, she didn't move.

Robbie's voice trembled as he spoke. "I'm sorry, Suze. I don't know what else to do. I just... I'll pray for you, okay?"

Without another word, Robbie turned and walked away, his head hanging low as his footsteps echoed in the damp, concrete surroundings of the flood channel. Suzie watched him go, her heart pounding, a feeling of utter devastation lapping at the edges of her mind.

"Come on, baby girl," Wonderman said gently.

Casting a final, lingering glance at Robbie, Suzie watched him ascend the steep bank of the flood channel. Then she too turned away, toward Wonderman and the drugs she knew he would give her, which she knew she would not refuse to take, no matter the consequences.

Chapter 16: Lessons

Suzie lay in the darkness, this strange underground world disintegrating around her. For days now, she hadn't moved from her grimy mattress, eating only a few chocolate bars left over from a recent garbage raid. One night, there was an argument. She sat upright, wondering if she'd finally lost her senses completely. Then, she recognized Lady's voice.

"You need to get her working. She's costing us being here and not working on her back… What's stopping you? You have feelings for the girl, don't you? I'm right, ain't I? You feel sorry for her. Or is it mere physical? Is that what it is, Wonderman, you low-down bastard—"

An angry, menacing voice cut in. It sounded like Wonderman, but Suzie'd never heard him rage like this before.

"Shut the fuck up! I decide what goes on down here, and when—I'll get her working when I'm good and ready…"

"Oh, will you," Lady sneered, "or is it that you don't yet have a hold over her like you do all the others… you can't threaten to expose her like you can the others. Anyone who was once *something* can be revealed to the world as nothing, less than nothing, in fact, but you don't know anything about her.

"Ain't it amazing how many'll hold on to their reputation, and hide down here, hoping the world will never find out? But I got some shit on you too, don't I, Wonderman?"

There were sounds of a struggle, and Suzie bolted upright. Could this be a chance to escape? She was fearful now, not knowing if this was reality or just another fabrication of her troubled mind, though it seemed real enough.

"Shut your fucking mouth. You're just a jealous whore, no different from all the rest…"

"Fucker, don't call me a whore…"

Was there more said, perhaps a scuffle? Suzie couldn't make anything out. They seemed to go silent, then Lady's voice, clear and languid, said: "I pray the storm comes quickly now, and washes you away…"

It took Suzie a moment to understand what Lady meant. It was now summer and the heat outside the tunnel was unbearable. Suzie had never associated Las Vegas with rainstorms before, though obviously, she was aware they occurred, living precariously in a flood defense channel. Still, it seemed so unlikely, but at the same time, there was talk of a thunderstorm approaching.

The flies were like a swarm. The stench of the tunnel and its inhabitants was overpowering. Suzie thought of her home in Oregon, a place that rarely, if ever, had heat like this. Oregon's climate was milder, with chilly winters for sure, and warm summers, but the desert here was extreme.

Her thoughts about home led her to consider Dana. She'd rarely allowed herself to do this, to feel the guilt she knew would threaten to overwhelm her if she let it. In all the months she'd been gone, she hadn't spoken to her mother. She called once—one rainy night in Oregon as winter set in, only weeks after she left.

She was at a bus station that happened to still have a working pay phone, an obsolete relic to most people now, but not to people like her. She'd been robbed days before, and her cell phone was one of the casualties. She remembered she had no idea where she was going to spend that night. She remembered feeling cold and hungry when she decided to make that call.

The phone line rang.

"Hello?" Dana's voice was hurried, as if she had run to take the call. Perhaps she knew. Perhaps she guessed it was Suzie at the other end.

Suzie had opened her mouth to speak, but no words came. Even now, she couldn't be sure what she'd wanted to say.

"Hello? Suzanne, is that you? Honey, is that you? If it is, come home. Please come home..." Dana was crying now. Suzie had never heard her mom beg before, and it frightened her.

"Suzanne. I know it's you. Honey, please, please come home...I love you. We'll work this out together. Please come..."

Suzie was beginning to stammer something when her time ran out, and the call ended with a series of beeps. She was left, holding the receiver, the last ebbs of possibility and hope draining out of her. Outside the bus station, the rain pelted down. She had no more money. Her last coin had been sucked in by the pay phone, leaving her feeling emptier than she ever had before.

Suzie had not tried calling again. She couldn't face the sound of her grief-stricken mother, the terrible knowledge of what she had done to her, the anger she still felt at her too. It was all so confusing, and so Suzie had slept somewhere that night, she couldn't remember where. Possibly hunched up on the ground of the bus station, or in a doorway somewhere, grabbing a few minutes sleep here and there, always hypervigilant to all those around her, those she knew would take any opportunity to harm her.

The next day, she had moved on, perhaps with one of the other lost souls who haunted the dark streets and alleys, perhaps alone. She'd moved on, but part of her remained at that pay phone, trying to say the words that would spirit her back home, and failing every time.

"Suzie, come on, come with us, we're going to look for food in the dumpsters."

It was Jazz speaking. Suzie had journeyed out of the tunnel to look at the sky, to try to see the storm clouds everyone was saying would gather soon. The sky was arching blue behind the normal haze of exhaust fumes. No clouds in sight.

"Judy says you need to start living again, and she's right. If you stay too long inside those tunnels, you'll never make it out." Jazz was smiling as he spoke to her.

Suzie shrugged, but managed a smile in return.

"Good!" beamed Jazz. "Girl, you need some flesh on them bones. You're looking skinny!" He chuckled good-naturedly as he walked beside her now.

"Where's Judy?" Suzie asked as they crawled through the hole already made in the chain link fence that ran above the road to prevent anyone from entering the channel.

Jazz's smile evaporated. "She's not good today."

Suzie wanted to know more, but Jazz's tone dissuaded her from inquiring further.

They navigated a large highway, walking along the inside shoulder for what seemed like miles, but was probably only a few hundred yards or so. The towering hotels of the Strip stood tall and unabashed in the distance. Suzie had to blink as she adjusted back to the light and fumes, the noise of the traffic, and the now unfamiliar rush of activity all around her.

"What do you mean, she's not good?" Suzie asked, her concern for Judy finally getting the better of her.

Jazz hesitated before replying, "Well, I don't know if you're aware how it works in the tunnel? All I'm saying is, there's a lot that Wonderman has to answer for. He gives all the drugs and then you have to go about earning them, or he…"

At this point, Jazz stopped talking and looked away.

"Or he what?" Suzie asked, thinking she may already know. She heard what Lady said earlier about Wonderman's leverage over those he pimped out.

"Or he nothing. Forget I said anything, Suzie. Come on, here's some bread and some fruit that don't look too bad…"

Later, inside the tunnel, Wonderman gripped Suzie's arm, practically dragging her to where Lady was set to begin one of her 'prayer' meetings. He held her firmly, not releasing his grip until Lady's sermon came to an end. Then, making sure everyone saw him, eyeing all the moles that stood watching, he stepped up onto an overturned crate, and began a sermon of his own.

Staring directly at Suzie, he raised his voice and declared: "No one up there cares about you." His eyes swept around the crowd like a hawk surveying its prey. Among the onlookers were Jazz and Judy, as well as Debbie and Steve, their expressions a mix of curiosity and concern. A few of the younger girls whom Wonderman had recently brought into the tunnels were there too, as were other hangers-on, pimps, pushers, and prostitutes.

"That's why we moles have to stick together," he continued. "All those do-gooders showing up outside to *help*"—this word he emphasized with particular disdain— "to them you're nothing, just a cog in their useful machinery. You think they want to help you?" Wonderman burst out laughing now, but the sound was unpleasant. It echoed around the tunnel.

"No! They have *jobs* because—we're—down—here. We're just the reason for their meetings, their committees, for the mayor to show *how much he cares*. The last thing they want is to really *help*. They don't give a shit about any of you!"

Here Wonderman paused for a moment, flashing a sinister smile.

"And now we have one more item of business to attend to," he said, gesturing for his burly enforcers to grab an unsuspecting drug addict near the front of the crowd. "Someone tried to abandon us last night…"

"No… no! Please," the addict shouted as they dragged him before Wonderman, "I'll pay you back. I'll pay you back tomorrow. Just give me one more day, please!"

Jazz and Judy exchanged worried glances.

Wonderman fixed his cold eyes on the terrified man.

"Tomorrow?" he sneered, his voice dripping with contempt. "You've had plenty of tomorrows, and yet here we are." He surveyed the crowd, looking at each mole one by one. "This is what happens when you don't keep your promises."

The addict struggled against the grip of the enforcers, but it was no use. His eyes were wide with fear, and tears streamed down his face. "Please, I swear I'll pay you back! I just need a little more time!"

Wonderman shook his head in mock disappointment. "I'm sorry, but time's up." He nodded to his enforcers, who grabbed the man by the hair and yanked his head back, exposing his vulnerable neck. Then, with a swift, brutal motion, Wonderman slashed out at him with a knife, cutting his losses while he cut the man's throat.

As the life drained out of the addict's body, Wonderman turned to face the onlookers, his icy blank expression remaining. "Let this be a lesson to all of you," he said, his voice low and menacing. "You'll all pay your debts to me one way or another."

At this, Suzie felt a wave of nausea course through her. She felt the urge to vomit, but there was too little in her stomach to expel.

The crowd of moles stared in shock and horror at the lifeless body. Some of them began to weep quietly, while others merely shrugged or looked away. As they all slowly dispersed, Jazz and Judy both took Suzie by the arms, attempting to support even her diminished weight as they began to stagger through the byzantine tunnels.

After what seemed like an eternity, Suzie heard Jazz's voice echo through the blackness.

"It's okay, baby. It's okay, we'll find a way to get out of here. We'll find a way…"

Part Three

The Storm Approaches

Chapter 17: Undercurrents

Thunder rumbled ominously across the darkening sky. Lightning flashed down from the heavens, yet still there was no rain. The Mole People had gathered outside in the desert. Lady stood at the forefront of the gathering, her arms raised, long, tangled dreadlocks cascaded down toward the parched earth.

"Hear this, hear us now," she intoned. "Keep us safe from the storm that approaches. Keep us safe from the torrents that could wash us all away. There will be downpours, we've seen them before, but we are the chosen, and we will not be swept away…"

Suzie watched with growing unease. Each breath she drew felt like inhaling hot, heavy air from a furnace, the oppressive heat intensifying around her. There was sweat trickling down her back even as lightning crackled.

"Stop the rains from coming. Stop them from falling, from sweeping us all away. We're not trash, we are the people who see everything, who live under the earth, far from the sinners above. We are the ones who see, so do not blind us. Guard us. Keep us safe!"

Lady kneeled and drew her arms over her head, sinking her forehead to the gravelly earth. The moles followed suit, their collective sighs and whispers creating an eerie drone as they lowered their heads to the ground, arms outstretched before them. As they did so, the slouching figure of Wonderman was revealed behind them, his sardonic grin still in place. He tipped his hat to Suzie before spitting, turning tail and walking, slowly, back to the flood channel. Two unfamiliar women detached themselves from the group, their gaze fixed on Wonderman as they trailed closely behind him.

More meat for his clients, Suzie thought, the nausea again threatening to overcome her.

She turned to her friends Judy and Jazz. Judy was jittery and restless, her face more haunted and gray than usual. The lines on her face seemed more pronounced, and she wiped at a sheen of sweat across her brow.

Judy was muttering to herself, and though her eyes were covered by a pair of sunglasses, Suzie could tell by her running mascara that she'd been crying.

"Judy, what is it? What's wrong?"

Jazz quickly grabbed Suzie's arm and took her aside.

"It's the anniversary…" he whispered.

"What do you mean?" Suzie asked, unable to tear her eyes off her friend.

"Her last ever concert. The one when it all went wrong. It was her crowning glory, but she was high as a bird up in the sky, she nearly didn't show up for it, and her manager had had enough. He knew she was using. They were calling her an addict, saying she was unreliable. She was ditched that night. He told her when she walked off stage. I don't think she's ever got over it…

"She loses it at this time of year. She takes anything she can. She's selling herself to that bastard Wonderman for more drugs. She don't even bother to ask for money anymore, she just scores a hit and that's enough for her. I hate him, but worse, I think I'm starting to hate her. She's destroying herself and there's nothing I can do about it."

Suzie stared at Jazz. The two scowling schoolgirls flanked him, their eyes narrowed. Suzie tried to ignore them, trying desperately hard to concentrate.

Those schoolgirls seemed to have grown bigger recently, though they were still the same age. Their size seemed to have expanded and grown, and their voices felt like they were getting louder every day. Suzie wanted to help her friend; she wanted desperately to express the affection she now had for her, but there was always something in the way, something inside her that halted the connection.

It wasn't just the voices, and the words they threw like knives at her. It wasn't just the people who weren't there but who appeared as real—the ones who truly existed, though? It was like she had an impenetrable glass screen between herself and the world, which no one could get past. The thought cast a shadow over Suzie's heart, as she realized her alienation only seemed to grow stronger with time.

"Suzie?"

"Sorry, Jazz, go on."

"There's nothing else to say, Suzie. I love her, but she's killing herself. I don't know what to do,"

Suzie took ahold of his hand, feeling the places where the three fingers once were, scarred stumps, at once the remnants of his musical career, and his ignoble destiny. She shook her head sadly. She knew she wouldn't be able to help Judy, or Jazz. Suzie was in the throes of drug addiction herself.

The tunnels seemed to do that to people. They wore you down. They got into your soul. Sure, you might have arrived broken and lost, but you soon found that your 'rock bottom' wasn't the lowest possible low. That journey began when you finally became a mole in the dark; when all hope was lost, when even the necessities of survival seemed too much to bear.

"I need to get Judy out of here. This tunnel is killing her. This life is destroying her, just like everyone else. You need to get out of here too, Suzie. This tunnel's like a vampire. It'll suck the life and spirit out of you."

Suzie knew this to be true, having already witnessed the powers Wonderman and Lady exerted in the shadowy confines of the tunnels. Somehow, they'd managed to unearth the deepest secrets of the moles, and their ultimate power lay in the ability to expose those secrets.

"There must be a way to take her away from—" Suzie started to say, but Jazz shook his head.

"I can't. We can't leave…" Just as Suzie began to ask why, Wonderman appeared again, his boots crunching down on the litter-strewn earth.

"I have something for you," he said to Jazz. Suzie looked at her friend and back to the man who brought her to this place. Was it her illness or were there undercurrents here she couldn't begin to fathom?

Later, she lay on her putrid mattress, listening to the sound of a piano playing somewhere in the far reaches of the tunnels. It was a disjointed noise, but it soothed her regardless, reminding her of her father.

Perhaps Jazz was playing, or perhaps not. She couldn't pick out the characteristic missing notes, which she would expect from Jazz's missing digits, but she didn't care. If it was her misfiring brain making the sounds, then she welcomed it. She welcomed the respite from the confusion, the pain, and the growing fear that gnawed at her in the dark.

Chapter 18: Judy

It was August now, and the sun bore down relentlessly on the scorched desert. Every day, Suzie joined the others, leaving the dark crevices of their makeshift dwelling to stare vacantly at the sky, to keep inquiring: "When will the rains come?"

Today was different, however. A more pressing concern arose. Blinking as she stepped outside, Suzie felt the rush of heat greet her, and immediately, Jazz approached.

"I can't find Judy. She's not in our place…"

"Maybe she went to look for food or get coffee?" Suzie looked around as if she expected Judy to appear miraculously out of the desert haze. Jazz's face was lined with worry. He frowned as he talked, and his movements were uncharacteristically jerky. Suzie suddenly felt a quiet dread, as if something terrible was inching inexorably toward them.

"She disappeared yesterday. She never came home last night. We'd had an argument, Suzie. It was bad. I tried to tell her we could leave. We shouldn't give a shit about Wonderman's threats—"

Suzie grabbed Jazz by the arm and took him aside, knowing they weren't alone;

there were always ears listening in this place. Ever since she'd arrived in the tunnels, she'd always felt like she was being watched. Maybe the paranoia was partly in her brain, but also, she wasn't stupid, she knew Wonderman and Lady had absolute dominion over the very air they breathed in those tunnels.

As tears welled up in Jazz's eyes and streamed down his face, Suzie felt a knot of panic tightening in her chest. In the short time she'd known him, Suzie had never seen Jazz lose his cool. His cheerfulness was omnipresent, or seemed to be, but this desolation, this was new. She dragged her hands through her hair, damp with sweat, coated in dust. Suzie couldn't remember how long it had been since she had a shower or washed her hair.

"What is Wonderman threatening? What does he have over Judy?" Suzie asked, though she was already sure she knew.

Jazz shook his head.

"It's nothing, not really. He says unless she sells herself for him, he'll go to the press and tell them where the vanished superstar singer has ended up. He says he'll expose her to the world, and she'll never live it down. Judy's got nothing except her reputation. I told her 'who gives a shit about Wonderman and his threats? He can't do nothing!'"

Jazz was working himself up now.

"It's the thing that'd hurt her the most—Judy Seal— now just a junkie living in some god-forsaken tunnel. But maybe that way she'd finally get some help. Maybe someone, some-where, might look on her kindly, might actually help her get free. That's why I said we should tell Wonderman to fuck off, and walk away. Let him do his worst, 'cause it sure as hell can't be worse than this."

"Listen, Jazz, we'll find her," Suzie said. "She must be further down in one of the tunnels. They say the rains are coming, so we need to find her quickly. I say we go back to your place first and see if she's shown up. Start the search from there if she hasn't."

Jazz nodded, wiped the tears from his grime-stained face. Suzie clasped his hand, the unsettling absence of several fingers always catching her off guard.

"I let her go after we argued, I let her go. I knew she was angry, but I didn't stop her…"

"We'll find her," Suzie said with a confidence she didn't feel. There were many parts of the tunnels she hadn't yet explored. Judy herself had warned her about them. They stretched miles beneath the city, housing not only the lost and homeless but also dangerous criminals lurking in the shadows, ready to pounce on the unsuspecting. If Judy didn't want to be found, then ultimately, they may have no hope.

Walking alongside Jazz, Suzie suddenly heard the stern man's voice shouting inside her head. He'd been quiet for a long time; Suzie was surprised to hear him. He was angry with her, furious in fact. Suzie darted her eyes around the tunnel, trying to ascertain if he was actually walking behind her, his voice seemed to boom so loudly against the concrete.

They're watching you. They know what you're up to. They'll come after you, they'll rip you to shreds. They've got hidden cameras all along the tunnel; they know all too well what you're doing...

Suzie swallowed. She tried hard to concentrate.

They can see you. They're watching you. When you're bad, they'll lock you up, and when they lock you up, they'll throw away the key. They'll never let you out...

"Suzie?" Jazz intoned, "we're here."

A bewildered expression on her face, Suzie met Jazz's gaze; a sudden jolt of awareness brought her back from the winding tunnels of her mind.

The voice didn't stop, but she managed to smile, managed to reassure her friend Jazz. He pulled back the curtain, and they saw Judy and Jazz's space in the beam of the flashlight. Everything was there—except Judy.

The shelf used as a kitchen counter, still had its bowl for washing cups, and a small heater to boil water. Their double mattress was made as neatly as the mess of sleeping bags and pillows allowed. The rack of clothes was still standing there, Judy's feather boa hanging conspicuously at one end.

"She's not here," Jazz said. "We have to go deeper in. Do you have a knife?" he added, his face set in a grim expression.

Suzie shook her head.

"Here, take this one, I'll take Judy's. She's left it here under her pillow," he said, reaching for the hidden weapon. Jazz's eyes widened with alarm as he handed Suzie the knife. "Without this, she's helpless. We need to reach her before something terrible happens."

Use the knife, Suzie. You know what to do. Take it, and take the pain away. You know you want to. Go on, take it, use it. Go on, do it…

Suzie grasped the knife, holding it fast, fighting the urge to draw it across her arm, to release all this tension, this build-up, this knot of thoughts and feelings that were out of her control. Her heart was thudding beat by beat, her hand trembled, but Jazz took no notice.

He beckoned her to follow him, and they started to make their way deeper into the dark recesses, further into the lawless maze. There were people lighting joints, laughing. A couple argued feverishly in the darkness. The sounds echoed and distorted. Suzie felt sick with fear. What awaited them down there, in the furthest reaches of the darkness?

They proceeded ever deeper into the void. Rats scuttled. Dank water dripped. Someone collided into Suzie, swearing bitterly, but Jazz shoved him to the side. Suzie swept her flashlight around until the beam found a haggard group, huddled in the far innards of the flood tunnel. The buzzing in her head grew and grew until it was unbearable.

You're a piece of shit. Kill yourself now. You deserve to die here with this scum. You're nothing. You're nothing. You're nothing!

Suzie let out a groan, but no one heard it. Here, in the furthest reaches of the tunnels, the stench was truly unbearable: with the squalid people, the dregs of drug use, accumulated trash, and human excrement. A dark figure coughed, and she saw two or three shadows, semi-conscious, stretched out against the graffiti-covered walls, ugly words, evil faces, demons that to Suzie, seemed to writhe and slither.

She clutched her head. The fear was overwhelming, every voice was screaming inside her now. She couldn't tell where the voices ended and the tunnel began. The air was wet and moldy, and she was convinced they'd finally arrived in the bowels of hell.

Suddenly, the beam of Suzie's flashlight landed on the slumped form of a woman, laying still. Jazz ran toward her, but time itself seemed to slow now as the awful dread took over. There was a cry from Jazz. Suzie lurched backward, finally comprehending the terrible reality, finally seeing what she'd hoped she would not see.

She knew Judy was dead before either of them reached her vacant body.

Chapter 19: Burial

"Judy! Baby! Come back! Don't die, you can't die and leave me here…"

Jazz tenderly held Judy's head, which dropped terribly to one side in his arms. He wept over her still body.

Suzie backed off, unsure what to do, unsure if this was real. The panic built inside her, and she couldn't tell if the sudden screaming she heard was coming from her own mouth, or those of her dreaded schoolgirls. In between sobs, Jazz shouted bitterly. He was cursing Wonderman, cursing the tunnels, cursing everything he knew in his grief and torment.

"If only the storms would come and wash away everyone, every last one of us. We deserve to die. We didn't save Judy. We didn't save her. No one should be left, no one…" He broke down in tears once again, until a desperate thought occurred: "Help me, Suzie. Help me lift her. We've got to get her home, see what we can do for her. She can't leave me."

Bewildered, Suzie wondered if Jazz knew Judy was gone or if this was all just a terrible dream. Maybe, in a moment, she'd wake up and find Lady handing her a delicious cup of coffee—always with two spoonsful of sugar—that haunting, absent smile on her face?

Gingerly laying down Judy's head, Jazz ran up to Suzie, grabbed her by the shoulders, and shook her desperately.

"Help me, Suzie! You've got to help me, for Judy's sake…"

She was backed up against the wall, screaming at the sight of Judy, seemingly oblivious to Jazz's pleas for help.

Jazz's voice cracked as he pleaded, "Suzie, please, I can't do this alone." Registering his desperation, Suzie snapped out of her daze and staggered forward.

"Of course, Jazz. We'll take her home together," she panted, her head throbbing still, though the screaming voice seemed to have stopped.

With great difficulty, they lifted Judy and carried her between them, and Suzie, now trembling, could feel the weight of their burden. This deep in the tunnel, the damp walls covered in grime, felt increasingly suffocating as they made their way through. The stench of mold and stale air filled Suzie's nostrils, making her breathing even more labored. As they carried Judy, the echo of their footsteps and ragged breaths in the narrow tunnel only amplified Suzie's sense of dread.

They finally laid her on the bed as gently as they could, careful not to let her head flop down, the weight of her surprising for such a slight frame. By now, word had gotten out and the other moles were starting to arrive, Lady among them.

"I'm sorry for your loss. She was called home by greater forces than we know or understand. I will gladly lead the ceremony," she said absently, before walking off.

Jazz didn't appear to have heard this. He lay by Judy's side, stroking her forehead, her cheek, her lips, whispering to the woman he loved, the woman who now lay cold and utterly unreachable in the black tunnel that was once her home.

The sky rumbled above Lady's head.

Dark clouds had gathered, but they only served to intensify the heat. Still, the rains held off as the Queen of the Apostles paused, stared upwards, blinking expectantly, as if she waited for God Himself to come down and bless her bizarre ceremony.

There was a hole dug roughly into the parched earth. Jazz worked through the night, knowing he didn't have the luxury of time. Those who died here, and it was not an uncommon event, were whisked off by the authorities—their names and circumstances never spoken of again.

It was anyone's guess where they went, but no one seemed to care anyway. Addicts died all the time from a simple overdose, from drugs cut with fentanyl, from malnutrition, dehydration, or in violent struggles with other moles.

Living here was a dangerous business. It was a lawless realm. A place where only the most lost and beaten dwelled; here there was little more than base survival at play. But through all this gloom and despair, a faint glimmer of friendship, of love, occasionally shone through, today in the few mourners who stood with Lady beside the hole that now contained Judy's body.

Jazz had dressed Judy in her finest attire, a deep red gown adorned with intricate beading, a final homage to her days on the stage. It was the same dress she'd worn for her last performance, as her addiction was laying waste to her career. The feather boa was wrapped around her shoulders, and her shoes were sky-high stilettos, though her frame was so gaunt that the dress sagged around her body, and the shoes were now too big for her withered feet.

Jump in! Jump in the grave! End it all now, Suzie Schizo! The pain and misery will be gone! You know you don't deserve to live; Judy was the best of everyone and she's dead. Now it's your turn. Just end it all, Suzie Schizo…

Suzie swallowed. She tried to concentrate her thoughts. She could feel Jazz beside her, his body shuddering as he cried softly.

Just jump in, Suzie! No one gives a shit if you're alive or dead. Dana abandoned you. Robbie abandoned you. You're just a burden, a fucking freak. No one cares, so why live? What's the point?

Suzie's knees buckled as she stood near the edge of the grave, her hands clenched into fists at her sides as she fought the urge to step forward and join her friend. It would take just a moment, a split second, to drop down into the grave. It wasn't too deep. She could lie down and let the earth swallow her up, fill her mouth, her nose. Soon she'd be smothered. Her breath, that ever-present nuisance which had stubbornly insisted on passing in and out of her lungs all these years, would soon be arrested.

As if Jazz read her troubled thoughts, he squeezed Suzie's hand.

"She loved you, you know. Oh, I know you didn't know each other for long, but she felt like a mother to you, or a big sister maybe. She was looking out for you, Suzie…" His voice cracked, as he struggled to find the words.

A wave of shame washed over Suzie, causing her cheeks to flush and her eyes to well up with tears. As she watched Jazz grieve, Suzie's heart clenched, realizing that what she secretly hoped for was the very thing causing his pain. Unable to control the voices in her head, Suzie gritted her teeth and lowered her gaze, trying to hide the guilt that consumed her as the voices continued their relentless chanting. Would she ever be free of them?

As Suzie stared into the pit that would soon be filled with dirt, her fingers brushed her own wrist, tracing the veins beneath her skin and yearning for the relief her friend had found. She could finally escape the cruelty her own mind dished out to her day in, day out. If she recalled that the voices subsided on her medication, then she didn't acknowledge that even to herself.

Next to Suzie, Debbie was crying. Steve stood beside her but his eyes were glazed over, as if he'd mentally checked-out long ago. There were a couple of the younger girls that seemed to come and go, burrowing in and then out of the tunnels, fellow moles for a few days or weeks before vanishing again. Suzie didn't recognize them, but she saw them both look over at someone who approached, from across the arid wasteland.

She looked up and saw the familiar shape of Wonderman, with his hat still set at its carefree angle. He chewed on something as he approached, then stopped at a distance. It took several minutes before Jazz noticed he was there. Just as Lady began her crescendo, the climax to her bizarre sermon, Suzie felt Jazz's hand clench.

"We beg you to take our Judy's spirit and receive her into the skies. We beg you to call her back to you for ever more, for she is one of the Mole People, and she is sacred…"

As Suzie frowned at Lady, who seemed transfixed by her own words, Jazz turned around and saw Wonderman standing a distance away, watching. Something inside Jazz seemed to explode.

"You bastard. You fucking bastard!" he muttered. Jazz looked back at Wonderman. He fidgeted, then, suddenly, he seemed to burst out from his grief, while Lady cried to the darkening heavens.

"Take our sister. Take her soul to the skies. Let her be reborn amid your love and wisdom…"

Jazz broke away from the group of moles, and marched across the parched desert toward Wonderman, whose composure didn't flinch. Some of the mourners were slow to catch on, blinded either by substances they'd taken or by grief, Suzie couldn't be sure, yet she saw Jazz walk away. She watched, torn between holding Jazz back and letting him confront the monster.

"Take her—" Lady stopped, aware finally that something was happening. She looked around, perplexed, as if coming around from a trance.

"You fucking bastard!" Jazz shouted. Above the din from the highway and the sound of the winds beginning to blow across the desert, his voice barely registered. He stopped directly across from Wonderman.

"You threatened to expose her, the woman I loved—and now she's dead! She coulda got away from this shithole, but you pimped her out, like you do all the women here, and she did it because all she had left was her reputation, her public image.

"You knew that, and you exploited her, you threatened to tell the press she was living here, and she's not the only one you've trapped like that. How dare you show your face at her funeral? How dare you come anywhere near us!"

Suzie instinctively moved to intervene. "Help me!" she cried, but before she could reach Jazz, two of Wonderman's enforcers grabbed him roughly. They pinned his arms behind his back, but in his incandescent rage he hardly seemed to notice.

"Fight me, you son of a bitch!" Jazz shouted, struggling against them, but the men had him overpowered.

Wonderman stood unmoved. The grin never left his face.

He watched, seemingly amused, as Jazz hopelessly attempted to stagger closer. Finally, Wonderman took action. He swung his fist, there was a sound like a dull thud, and Jazz fell to the ground. It was efficiently done. Despite the impact, Jazz was already pulling himself to his feet, one hand on his stinging cheek. Wonderman gestured for his goons to step back.

"Why couldn't you just let Judy go? What did it matter to you whether you kept her or not? I loved her. I loved Judy and now she's dead because of you…"

Jazz was sobbing now, slumped down on the ground again. Suzie wrapped her arms around Jazz, pulling him close, trying to end the confrontation for her friend's sake.

"Stop! Stop! He's my friend… Jazz, you have to stop now, you have to calm down. This won't bring Judy back, and you don't want an enemy like Wonderman." Cradling Jazz in her arms, she looked over at the fiend known as Wonderman.

"You as good as murdered her," Jazz spat for the final time at Wonderman, who rubbed his fist, then set his hat back on his head as if nothing of importance had happened.

Suzie looked down at her friend. "Come on, get up. We need to get away from here." She had to half-drag Jazz back to his dwelling inside the tunnel. She saw Wonderman staring after them, smiling still.

"Why did you do that? He's your enemy now!" Suzie panted as they collapsed in Jazz's place. "He slashed that man's throat just yesterday."

"I couldn't help it," Jazz said. "I hate him. I hate him for everything. I couldn't stop myself, Suzie. I don't care if he finishes me off soon, I had to do it for my girl. She's dead, Suzie, Judy is dead and she died in the tunnel. She'll hate that. She was so scared of dying here and I always told her, no, I *promised* her, I'd get her out before that happened. Look what happened to my promise. I failed her. Suzie, I failed her so bad. I don't know if I can ever forgive myself."

Jazz began to weep, his anger melting into pure grief.

Outside, the first drop of rain was released from the sky. It spiraled downward, hitting the ground silently. Then came another, and another. The rains had begun.

Chapter 20: Escape

"Do you think her spirit's gone up to the sky, like Lady said?" Jazz murmured.

Suzie pulled herself onto her elbow and looked down at her friend, his face outlined by candlelight. It was hours later, and they were sitting in Jazz and Judy's place, talking, and crying, the shock still evident on their faces.

"I don't know. My mom says there's a heaven," Suzie offered.

"You've never talked about her before, what's her name?" Jazz asked.

Suzie closed her eyes as a wave of memories washed over her. Dana. Her name invoked a bittersweet ache in her heart, a reminder of the life she had left behind. But she was the reason Suzie had to leave, or one of them anyway. If she cared she'd have been here by now. Robbie came…

Suzie realized she couldn't remember how long it'd been since her boyfriend appeared, then finally abandoned her forever. It didn't matter anyway. She told herself she didn't care, but if that was true, then why did it still hurt so bad?

"Her name was Dana."

"Dana. That's a nice name. She must be missing you?" Jazz said. He was clutching one of Judy's stuffed animals, one of the few she'd rescued from city dumpsters, discarded and abandoned, just like the moles in the tunnels.

Suzie shrugged again, changed the subject as a lump came into her throat. She didn't like to think of Dana, or home. It was like she was living a whole different life now, and the past was only something that could drag her further down. The candle flickered, and they both turned to its small light.

"Well, I wonder if that was Judy's way of saying hello," Jazz mused, his eyes glistening with unshed tears. "She didn't stand a chance in here. She was too soft, too loving. She shoulda been shining on a stage somewhere, not dying here and buried with the trash."

Suzie bit her lip, lost for words. She hugged herself tightly, her gaze distant as she wondered who would mourn her if she died. Maybe nobody would; the voices in her head were probably right about that.

"Did you ever see her sing?" Suzie asked.

"Never on stage. I met her after she'd lost everything," Jazz replied. "I guess I wanted to save her, or rescue her, or some dumb thing like that. I couldn't even save myself, so how could I save her? But we had something good together—before this place took that too..."

Jazz sat up suddenly, taking a hold of Suzie's hands.

"I've gotta get outta here," he said, determination in his voice. "And you should come with me. There's no life for us here, you can see that, Suzie. Wonderman will turn on you one day soon. He'll wake up from whatever spell you've put on him and he'll demand his 'payment' for protecting you.

"The clock is counting down for you, Suzie. You have to leave with me. We could go tonight. No one will think to look for us while we're all still shocked about Judy."

Suzie sat up, frowning. "Where would we go? We might end up some place worse. At least here, we know what we're dealing with. We know how this place works. We know where to find food and we can sleep off of the streets..."

Jazz stared into her eyes, his expression a mix of desperation and fear.

"Suzie, this place is cursed. It'll be the end of you soon, I know it."

She shifted on the bed, her brow furrowed with unease as she instinctively backed away a little from her friend. "They'll come after us. Or we'll end up somewhere that could be worse. I'm sorry, Jazz. I'm just not sure."

"I'll protect you, Suzie. I'll look after you, and I'll make it up to Judy that way. Can't you see, we've got no other choice?

"I don't know what they'll do to us if we stay, but I'm not welcome here now after I went for Wonderman like that in front of everyone. You came and supported me. He won't like that.

"He'll see that as a betrayal—and he'll make you pay for it. You're his enemy too now…"

Jazz's eyes widened, his voice laced with urgency. He leapt up off the ground, his hands trembling as he seized an old backpack and hastily stuffed it with clothes and essentials: a flashlight, a couple sodas, his knife and some t-shirts.

"You're not safe here. Neither of us are. Face it, Suzie, we don't have a choice."

Outside, the once gentle raindrops had transformed into a relentless downpour. Water cascaded from rooftops and pooled on the dark, glistening streets. Topsiders had retreated to their hotels to wait out the storm, which could last for days, but down in the tunnel, the moles were still unaware.

Just as Suzie was about to respond, a sudden noise startled them both. Lady's voice echoed through the tunnel, and Jazz swiftly hushed Suzie before she could reply.

"Shhhh. She may not know we're here…" Jazz whispered, his words barely audible. Suzie watched as he blew out the candle, casting them into an instant, suffocating darkness. They both peered out of the curtain, and saw a shape about the size of Lady, her braided dreadlocks silhouetted by the light of her flashlight. Standing with her were two smaller figures, one of whom was a girl who couldn't be more than fourteen years old.

"You've come to the right place, baby girl. We'll look after you. We just gotta go see the man in charge down here, and get you settled in…" Lady's voice echoed through the tunnel.

Suzie felt the nausea threatening again, fighting to overcome her, but this time she pushed it back. She had to push it back for Judy's sake.

"I'll be back, I promise," Suzie hissed, as she crept away. Jazz grabbed for her hand, a panicked look in his eyes.

"What you doin', girl? You don't go sneaking around Wonderman down here…" he said.

Don't listen to him. Don't listen to anyone, said the voices, *no one cares about you. You're just another useless mole…*

"I'm going. Don't worry, I'll be fine. I just need to go…" Suzie whispered, shaking her hand free.

Could Wonderman and Lady really be low enough to pimp out a fourteen-year-old girl? Suzie needed to know for sure. She needed to hear it for herself. Suzie cautiously trailed behind Lady and the girls, her pulse quickening as they ventured deeper into the darkness. As Lady took a left turn, Suzie's gut twisted in apprehension, realizing they were heading toward the space she shared with Wonderman.

Suzie kept back, but she could hear every word they said, the tunnel echoing the sound of their voices.

"Well now, who have we here?"

Wonderman's voice was a drawl. Suzie managed to dampen down the chatter inside her head, hearing him clearly. Somehow, her focus was laser-sharp now, and it felt good, it felt like power.

"I brought you Josie and her friend. Josie's a peach, a real looker. Turn around, baby girl, and show Wonderman what you got…"

Baby girl…

There was a pause, then Wonderman spoke again.

"You're sure as hell a beauty, though you're young, ain't ya?"

There was no sound from the girl, but perhaps she nodded or made some gesture.

Lady continued: "She's perfect. I told you so. She's new to the city, and she needs protection. I've told her we can look after her. We'll keep her safe, won't we, Wonderman?"

"Course we will. Now, Josie, if you're kind to me, then I'll be kind to you. That's how it works down here. We'll keep you safe, but you need to know the rules. D'you know how to make a man happy?"

The girl's voice, when it came, was clear enough, though it bore the apparent innocence of a teenager, barely a woman biologically. "Yeah, I know how to do that."

Suzie shuddered. That girl was too young for this, for the bravado and bullshit. She was probably a runaway, perhaps from an orphanage, a dysfunctional family, or some other shit she'd had to deal with, or gotten herself into. Then came that familiar scent of tobacco—with the chemical stench mixed in.

"Have a smoke on this, beauty. Let's be friends, then we'll see…"

Lady laughed at something, and Wonderman replied, but his voice was muffled now. Suzie realized it was time to go before she was discovered.

She crept away, went back and found Jazz, who'd finished packing his things by now and was awaiting her return.

"I won't stay here any longer. Wonderman blackmailed my baby, but he ain't got nothing on me. Suzie, come with me. If you stay down here, you're trapped as surely as a bird in a cage."

Suzie stared back at him. Hearing Josie's slight voice echoing in her head louder and louder, she knew it was time to leave. She was seized suddenly by a desire to get out, a desire to escape, no matter the cost. At once, the months of claustrophobia and blackness, the dirt and fetid air, were unbearable. She was almost shocked by this strength, this sudden craving to be free.

"I'll come," she said, "but we have to save that girl. He's going to pimp her out. He's already getting her on drugs. Jazz, we have to help."

"No, Suzie, if we're going to do this, it has to be now. We can't save anyone here, except maybe ourselves. Come on, I'm sorry for her but we have to go."

Jazz took Suzie's hand and pulled her along through the tunnel, passing by other mole people. There was a flurry of movement now. People seemed to be packing their things. Perhaps they were escaping too.

"Come on!" Jazz said, sensing Suzie's hesitation. He looked around at her, wondering why she'd stopped abruptly in her tracks.

At the mouth of the tunnel, just when freedom was finally within reach, a figure stepped forward. It was a woman, and she was soaking wet. For a moment, Suzie thought she was hallucinating.

This woman's figure, her stance, the way she peered into the gloom: all unmistakable.

It was her mother.

Chapter 21: Revelation

As lightning danced across the desert skies and dark clouds hovered, thunder rolled and boomed, startling Suzie. Hiding away with Jazz in the aftermath of Judy's funeral, she had no idea the rains had finally begun, lashing down onto the decadent denizens of Las Vegas.

"Suzanne, is that you? My God…" Dana was soaked to the bone. Her ordinarily immaculate hair was straggly and wet, dripping onto her clothes. Her jacket was missing, and her blouse and skirt were drenched.

Suzie peered out at her suspiciously.

"Suzanne?"

Dana stared back with equal suspicion. This couldn't be her Suzie—the same girl who'd run away all those months ago. The emaciated woman in front of her had deep black shadows under her eyes, and a cagey, animal-like look about her. What had she done to herself? Dana realized yet again that she had failed her, she'd utterly failed her.

"It *is* you. Oh my God, look at you… Robbie was right, you're here, living in this place…I wasn't sure at first, but when I saw your eyes…"

"Mom?"

"Oh Suzanne, I'm sorry, I'm so, so sorry. How did this happen? How did you end up here with these people?"

It was Suzie's turn to step back.

"Some of *these people* are my friends," she said, defensively. Suzie was wary now, on her guard. Why was Dana here? If she thought she could just swoop in like Robbie, and then vanish again forever, Suzie wanted nothing more to do with her. Already, her back was up like a frightened cat, its hackles rising.

Suzie turned to go, but where? Wasn't she about to leave the tunnels? And why were the voices in her head, the school-girls, the stern man, why were all of them now shouting wildly, starting to hurl insults, chanting derisively as her head pounded?

"Suzanne, honey, don't go. Please don't go. I've driven so far to find you. I haven't slept for months. I know it was all my fault. I know that I should've told you, that I've kept so much from you. You're right to hate me, or whatever it is you feel, but please, please don't go—"

Dana's voice broke off. She began to sob, holding out her arms just as she used to do when Suzie was a baby. Every cell in her body yearned for forgiveness, yet she could see she'd startled the young woman.

It took a moment for Suzie to understand the words, for them to make sense to her.

"What do you mean, you should've told me? Told me what?"

Suzie stood stock-still, her mind racing as she tried to decode her mother's words. *Is this really happening?* she thought, aghast at seeing Dana cry. *What could be so important that she came all this way to tell me? What has she hidden from me?*

Even though the voices were still hurling insults at her, there was a part of her mind that was strangely calm. This part was focused now on every word her mom was saying. This part knew there was something more at stake here, some hidden meaning or secret that just needed to be deciphered, unraveled to make sense. It felt imperative, and so Suzie didn't run away. She stayed, but like an animal cornered, every sense bristling.

"Robbie told me you were here. He told me to forget you, that you were beyond saving, but I couldn't just leave you. I had to come and see for myself. What's happened to you?

Oh, my love, my love, what have I done? What have I done? I should've told you everything, about your father—and your mother…"

Dana stepped closer. Her skin felt ice cold despite the humidity of the storm.

"What are you talking about?" Suzie asked, this time speaking harshly.

With tears streaming down her cheeks and a quiver in her voice, Dana's grief-stricken face crumpled as she uttered the words that would shatter Suzie's already fractured world into smithereens:

"I think you've always known it deep down. I think part of the reason you've been so ill is because of the lies I've told you, lies you've sensed even as a small child. I can't live with myself anymore, Suzanne. I have to tell you the truth."

"The truth about what, Mom?" Suzie was close to yelling now. Had Dana gone insane? Was it Suzie's fault because she left her? A tsunami of emotions hit the young woman: guilt at having left, unease at what Dana was saying, anger at this humiliating scene unfolding in the dank tunnel, the moles watching.

The sound of the rain punctuated their voices. It beat down, pooling treacherously at their feet, but neither woman seemed to notice.

Dana's face was a picture of misery.

"Suzanne, you must have guessed? Surely, you must know in your heart that I'm not your mother?" Her voice cracked. She stepped forward, holding out her hand, an empty gesture that Suzie promptly ignored.

Suzie's eyes widened and her body tensed as if she had turned to stone, her breath caught in her throat and her heart pounding as Dana's words echoed and swirled around her.

She knelt, then suddenly, leaned over and vomited. She wiped her face with her arm and looked over at the older woman.

"I don't understand—"

"I think you do," Dana said, miserably. "I think you understand everything, and always have. Suzanne, your mother died when you were very young. I met your father when he was grieving, and when we knew our feelings for each other, we decided to wait to tell you. But then he died, and I couldn't find the words. You'd lost both your parents, and there was no family to take you in. You would've had no one.

"I couldn't tell you the truth because by then, you always called me 'Mom'. I thought I would break you into pieces if I told you the truth, that you were an orphan. I was wrong to think that, I know that now…"

Dana's voice trailed off as she began to see the impact her words had on Suzie. The young woman had turned even more pale, if that was possible. Her breathing was shallow, she was looking around trying to figure out if she'd heard her correctly, if it wasn't some other voice somewhere, if what she said was true or not.

She didn't know what to do. She didn't know what to say. Before she could move, Dana gripped her hand. Suzie tried to free herself but then she felt something inside her palm, an envelope, folded up, beginning to unfurl. Dana let go of her and stepped back. She watched Suzie warily, as if she were an undetonated bomb that could go off without warning.

Suzie was trembling now. She felt sick and scared, like a small child again. All she could think, was that she has to get away from this woman, this person who was not her mother. She remembered in her dreams that scented kiss, those ruby red lips, and wondered if she'd always known, and had been too afraid to admit the truth.

The buzzing in her head grew. All thoughts of escaping with Jazz had disappeared. Suzie stumbled away, further and further into the blackness of the tunnel, still grasping the envelope, a desperate wailing now escaping from her lips.

147

Chapter 22: Trapped

Suzie's heart hammered in her chest as she desperately gulped in the dank air. Panting, she continued to run through the tunnel, not caring where she would end up. The stench grew worse and worse as she ran, stumbling on discarded trash, knocking against moles here and there, slumped over or cooking up their drug of choice.

The damp, slimy walls of the tunnel seemed to close in around her. Dodging the swipes of several people, she pressed on, venturing deeper and deeper into the tunnel. Then, she realized that people had started to go in the opposite direction, panic in their eyes as they snatched at their possessions, scurrying out of the tunnel as the rains kept falling, as the floodwaters rose relentlessly.

Suzie knew the floods could wash away everything—lives included—but right now, she didn't care. Her thoughts careened chaotically through her head, like a train off its tracks. Her mind felt separate from her body. It seemed to shout at her from outside her, the mental chatter enduring with every frantic step she took.

Her whole damned life had been a lie. Nothing had been real.

No wonder I'm so messed up, she thought, and that only fueled her flight all the more. Her feet pounding against the concrete, she wanted to run and run forever, but her weakened legs eventually gave out, leaving her collapsed on the ground, alone in the dark, far, far into the tunnels. She vomited again, and curled up on the floor, her body heaving with uncontrollable sobs.

It was then that she saw him in the blackness. Her father emerged, sat at the piano, and the first note rang out; that melancholic sound lingering in the humidity of the tunnel. Then, a cascade of notes followed, echoing through the serpentine depths, disappearing into the stifling blackness. Gentle at first, they danced and flitted as the music built, as the tempo increased, as the loneliness of the piece filled the hollow reaches of the tunnel.

Suzie recognized Chopin's *Ballade Number 1*, her father's favorite piece of music, the one that always took her back to those Sunday afternoons at home when she would listen to him play. So long ago. So much had happened, yet she felt just like she did then: transfixed with a kind of yearning for something just out of reach. She remembered every note as if each one was a part of her soul.

Herb was sitting at his old piano, his hands moving deftly, his eyes shut in concentration as he played. She was confused. The piano sat in the living room at home, and yet she knew she was not there. Suddenly, the damp, the heat, the sour stench all vanished and she was transported back into her memories, her childhood, or part of it anyway. She wanted to stand up, to walk over to him and place a single hand on his thin shoulder, but she would risk him turning around to smile at her, and in doing so, stopping.

She watched in wonder as the blue-veined hands, so awkward in life, so fumbling, moved like they used to, with impeccable timing, with deft assurance. Their elegance, the way they glided over the keys, with gentle grace, was spellbinding.

The music echoed and distorted in the tunnel, notes bounced and reverberated off the concrete walls—muffled at times— then louder, then softer. He played on, his head dipping toward the piano, listening intently like a bird, his head cocked to the side, utterly transfixed by the sounds; their depth, their longing. She watched, silently. Tears cascaded down her cheeks, leaving wet trails in their wake.

From deep within the blackness, she didn't hear the rolling thunder overhead, nor the sound of rain lashing the desert. She didn't see the lightning as it scarred the sky, electrifying the desert, compelling people to run for shelter. She didn't notice the black clouds as they moved overhead with surprising speed, bringing with them the storm that the sky had promised for days and weeks now.

She heard none of this, deep within the labyrinth, as the tunnels breathed their own sour air, as the clouds emptied their cargo, as water hit the desert plains, the dwellings, the roads, hotels, and glimmering casinos with torrential force. Only the sound of the piano and the sight of her father filled her heart and mind as the first trickles of water began to lap ominously at her feet.

Chapter 23: Floral Scent

Between ebbing sobs, Suzie felt the envelope in her hand as if it had just been placed there. With trembling hands, she opened it, careful not to drop the contents. She rummaged in her pocket for the flashlight and switched it on. The envelope contained a small faded photograph of a young woman with raven black hair. Suzie could feel the woman's joy radiating from her face as she cradled a chubby-cheeked baby. Who was this woman, so young and happy looking?

In her heart, Suzie knew. It was the woman with the floral scent, the one who kissed her pudgy cheeks as a baby. It had been so easy over the years to think she was delusional or hallucinating, instead of realizing it was an actual memory of her real mother.

How much of her mind's games and tricks had, in fact, been recollections? How much of the madness thrown at Suzie by her own brain, had been the truth? She couldn't say, and the enormity of her questions weighed heavy. Too much had happened to untangle it all now.

At the same time, her father's music built and built, at first slowly and gracefully, then with an urgency that used to surprise her, but felt appropriate now. Suzie was barely breathing. She let the sounds roll over her, feeling the years wind back to the beginning, knowing the truth at last.

Suzie didn't notice the alarming speed at which the water rushed through the tunnel. Where only minutes earlier it pooled at her feet, it now reached up to her knees. The water churned, carrying with it broken bottles, scraps of paper, and other debris that clung to her skin like oil.

The piano's melody fought against the roaring floodwaters, its notes straining to be heard above the tumultuous sounds of the rushing water, but she couldn't see her father anymore.

There was no piano.

There was no sound except the ever-present voices that said over and over: *They lied to you. They didn't ever love you. If they'd loved you, they'd have told you the truth. No one wants you, you fucking weirdo. You're better off dead.*

A bitter mix of betrayal and disbelief gnawed at Suzie's heart as she began to understand the extent of the deception that had surrounded her entire life.

Suddenly, there was a loud scream, and the danger finally registered with her.

The flow of water had quickly transformed into a violent torrent, the murky water now waist-high and rising at an alarming rate. The remaining moles were scrambling to save themselves and their meager possessions from the merciless onslaught of water. Makeshift shelters were ripped apart, and debris swirled within the churning waters, creating a deadly whirlpool of sharp, jagged objects that threatened to injure or trap anyone caught in their path.

Struggling to advance against the powerful current, Suzie found it increasingly difficult to maintain her footing as she tried to make her way through the disorienting whirl of water and debris.

The screaming grew louder.

The sound was unmistakable now.

Dana.

Suzie turned to the direction of the noise.

Dana screamed again.

Suzie began to push herself toward the sound, the beam of her flashlight bouncing off the foaming water. She stumbled through all the trash, which swirled amid the deluge. Her instincts told her where she must go, and she found the strength to keep going until she reached Wonderman's quarters.

"Stop, stop! Leave me alone! I only want Suzanne…"

By flashlight, Suzie saw Dana was pinned to the wall, whimpering, begging. Wonderman was holding a knife to her throat. He flinched at Suzie's flashlight, now shining full-on at him, but he didn't turn around.

"Tell me, what do you know about Suzie that made her run like that. Tell me, or I'll rearrange your face… I have to say, it don't look much like Suzie's—" Wonderman said with menace.

"Back off, Wonderman," Suzie ordered. She was holding the knife Jazz gave her, the knife she'd carried with her since that terrible day. She was shaking both with cold and with fright, but the blade, at least, was steady. "Our business is none of your fucking concern. Get away from her, now."

Her voice was strong. She shined the light straight at Wonderman, who grimaced briefly.

"But why should I do that, baby girl? Why wouldn't I want to know your secrets? I knew there was something about you…" He played at Dana's throat with the knife. "You're not some lowly girl on the run. You've got money. I wonder how much it'll take to set your mommy free…"

Dana shut her eyes. She was whimpering again now.

"So, this is how you keep ahold of all your little moles, huh?" Suzie said. "By getting them to tell you things, by blackmailing them? We all have secrets, Wonderman. I'm guessing you have a few yourself."

Wonderman snorted at this.

"You're just a piece of shit, aren't you, Wonderman? So, it's on to kidnapping now?"

He turned around, still holding the knife to Dana's throat.

"It sure is, baby girl. You'll be worth keeping ahold of, I think." He laughed, but his eyes remained cold and calculating.

Suzie stepped forward, the blade of her knife glinting in the beam of the flashlight. Before she could reach Wonderman, she was seized from behind.

"What the—?"

The sharp cold of a steel blade at her throat told her she was now just as helpless as Dana.

"Let go of the knife like a good girl…"

It was Lady's voice.

"You bitch," Suzie said.

"Just let go of the knife…" Lady repeated.

Suzie looked over at Dana hopelessly. Dana's eyes widened, darting desperately between Suzie and Lady. Her mouth was moving, perhaps in prayer, but no sound that Suzie could hear came out. They were alone now, defenseless, lost. Lady pushed the knife further against her throat. Any closer, and she'd start to bleed.

Suzie saw she had no choice. She dropped her knife into the rushing water, watching the current swirl it away, forever out of reach.

Lady shrugged at the danger unfolding. "Nature's way of cleaning up once in a while…"

The trickle had become a torrent. Neither Lady nor Wonderman seemed to care. Lady pushed Suzie against the wall.

"I knew from the minute you got here, you'd be trouble," Lady said. "I told him to get rid of you, to throw you out, but he wouldn't listen. He liked the look of you. He was saving you for himself, of course. Now, I couldn't let that happen, could I? I couldn't let some high-class girl saunter in here and take my man from me, 'specially one with problems like yours, with *madness* like yours…"

"You just couldn't find a way to use it against me," Suzie said, turning and spitting right in Lady's face.

"You'll fucking pay for that—"

But before Lady could finish her threat, another voice pierced the dark.

"She won't be paying for anything. Drop the knife."

Chapter 24: Reckoning

For a moment, no one spoke. Suzie looked back, half expecting to see her father's face, those kind eyes, that absolute sense of right and wrong.

Instead, she was confused when she saw Robbie, his face illuminated by his own flashlight. He'd appeared out of the gloom, and was standing behind Wonderman. He wasn't alone. She could see Jazz struggling against the water.

"I wouldn't use that knife," Robbie said, as if he had all the time in the world. "There are plenty of witnesses here, and the cops are on their way. Apparently, they've been hoping to lock you two up for a while now. Jazz told them where you bury the bodies."

Suzie blinked. She looked over at the man she ran away from all those months ago, but this time he met her gaze.

"I'm here for you, Suzie. I let you down before, but I'm gonna make it up to you," he said.

All of them stood still, frozen for what seemed like ages but was really only a few seconds, the water churning around them. The flood had risen fast, and it was only getting worse as each moment passed.

"Drop the knife, Lady," Jazz said, stepping forward. "Just drop it now, and let's get the hell out of here." His face reflected the fury of them all. He seemed to stand a foot taller now.

Lady looked to Wonderman, who stared back at her, his eyes glinting black in the darkness. The filthy water gushed through the tunnel with a deafening roar.

"We need to get out of here, the water's rising. The rain isn't stopping anytime soon. We could all drown!" Robbie yelled above the din of the rushing flood waters. "Let go of her," he said to Lady. With difficulty, he stepped forward against the current of the water. A lounge chair went past now, narrowly missing Suzie who was now drenched.

Lady glanced at the rising water and the determined faces around her before shrugging, taking a step back, and dropping the knife with a resigned smile. The water was already swirling against their torsos. Lady shoved Suzie forward as a parting gesture, and Suzie waded as fast as she could toward Robbie. He turned now to Wonderman, who was still holding his knife up to Dana's throat.

"Time's up," he said. "Let her go."

The two men eyed each other, as the water continued to rise precariously.

"We need to get out of here. Please let me go," Dana whimpered, her eyes darting between the two men.

Robbie glared at Wonderman. "You remember the name Megan, don't you?"

At the mention of the name, Wonderman's eyes widened slightly, a flicker of surprise—or was it fear?—passing through them.

"Megan," Robbie continued, "They found her in that grave too."

Wonderman's face paled, and then Suzie saw it. She saw the hesitation, the doubt where before it was all bravado and menace. Wonderman didn't know what to do.

"Let my mother go," Suzie shouted, glancing at Dana as she spoke, knowing the import of her words. Dana looked at her, quizzically. Briefly, they smiled at each other.

"Let my mom go," Suzie repeated, nodding at Dana. In that moment, as the danger increased, as the tension soared, Suzie grasped what she should have known all along. It didn't matter who the woman with the perfume and the red lips was to her. Dana would always be the only mother she had ever truly known, who she ever would know.

Wonderman smiled as tears slid down Dana's face. He looked back and forth at them, his knife blade still held fast against her skin. One deft move and he could slice her throat open.

Everyone was still.

"Kill her and you'll rot in jail for the rest of your goddamn life," Robbie said.

No one said anything.

All were thinking, what came next?

The tunnel answered quickly.

The water surged with a roar, knocking Lady over as Jazz threw himself against the tunnel wall. Meanwhile, Robbie staggered, desperately holding onto Suzie.

Wonderman hadn't seen it coming.

With a startled shout, he was thrown into the swirling depths, knocking into Jazz and almost throwing him into the current too. Jazz yelped and bent over double as Wonderman disappeared into the frothy waves. Dana staggered, holding her throat. There was blood there from the blade's touch. Suzie threw herself toward Dana, dragging them both to the wall.

"We need to get out of here. Fast! Hold onto each other, and follow me..." Jazz said, struggling toward the tunnel entrance. Robbie grabbed Suzie, who now had ahold of her mother, and together, they moved as one toward the exit.

Just then, Suzie turned and saw Lady.

Her eyes were wide with terror. She was floundering, desperately grasping onto a ripped curtain, her knuckles white, as the cold, raging floodwaters threatened to sweep her away.

Suzie relished the thought of turning away from her, of saving just herself and her mother, of leaving Lady there to drown. There was another great rush of water, and Lady cried out. But then, inconceivably, Suzie threw herself toward Lady and grabbed her hand. Together, they were swept away under the torrent.

"Suzie!" Dana screamed, at a loss for why she would help this woman.

Robbie took Dana's arm and pulled her toward the exit.

"Get out of here, I'll get her back," he yelled.

The flashlights had been swept out of their hands almost immediately.

The tunnel was black as night now.

Gasping for breath, Suzie and Lady fought against the current that crashed against them. They kicked out at the water, feeling themselves being dragged along against their will. The terror was all-consuming, but then Suzie felt her body thrown against the wall. Gripping ahold of Lady's arm, Suzie helped her scramble upright, and they pressed themselves flat against the graffiti-daubed concrete.

"Where's Wonderman?—Where is he?" Lady blurted out, struggling for air. Just as she spoke, the water dragged her under again.

"Keep ahold of me!" Suzie shouted back.

What are you doing, Suzie Schizo? Why are you helping her? a voice intoned. It was the stern man inside her head. He admonished her even as she grasped Lady's hand. *Stupid Suzie Schizo strikes again. This bitch would've sold you as a whore.*

Suzie delved deep within herself, grasping for the answer.

I know, but I can't just let her die. The others came back for me, even though I didn't deserve to be saved, so I've come for her, even though she sure as hell doesn't deserve it either.

Suzie was aware she was replying to the voices in her mind now. *Almost like I'm crazy*, she thought. Somehow, right now, she didn't care. A mattress hurtled past, barely missing both of them.

Then out of the darkness, came Robbie.

"Grab my arm!" he shouted.

Clinging to each other for dear life, every step through the raging flood waters was a precarious dance with disaster, their hearts pounding in their chests. Every second felt like it would wash them away; every second felt like an hour until they finally reached the entrance of the tunnel.

Water was everywhere. The once-small channel had transformed into a treacherous, fast-flowing river. With desperate determination, they clawed their way to the bank, narrowly escaping the relentless current's grip.

Drenched and covered in muck, Suzie spotted Dana and the others, a wave of relief washing over her as she realized they were safe.

As soon as they finally stepped into the refuge of the street, Lady threw off Suzie's hand and staggered away without a word. Suzie let her go.

"How did you know to come?" Suzie said when Robbie enveloped her in his arms.

"I heard the floods were coming. I guessed you'd be in danger so I called your mom. I told her I was coming for you to get you out, whatever it took. I abandoned you before, and I couldn't live with myself. So Dana and I came up with a plan. We didn't know the rains would start when they did, but we knew it'd be soon. We knew the danger was greater every day you stayed in here, so we came to look for you together."

Robbie tucked a piece of hair behind Suzie's ear.

"I came for you, Suzie. I knew I was wrong, leaving you here. I could never live with myself if I hadn't tried to get you out…"

Finding herself unable to speak, Suzie stood there in silence, the exhaustion and shock finally setting in. As she began to shake violently, a police officer handed her a foil blanket. An ambulance, flanked by several police cars with flashing lights, stood nearby. Paramedics were already assessing Dana. Thankfully, the knife only left a surface wound which was being treated. Suzie walked over to her, this woman who had risked everything to find her.

"You called me 'Mom'," was all Dana said, smiling as a paramedic dabbed at the cut on her neck. Dana was trembling too.

Suzie nodded, her voice firm yet gentle, "That's because you are."

They smiled at each other, their faces weary, their clothes soaked.

Suzie found she couldn't speak further, but she didn't need to.

As Suzie looked over at Lady being examined by a paramedic, she felt a strange mix of sympathy and anger, wondering if Lady could ever change. She was turning her face away, gesticulating wildly, and Suzie's hope that she could now be truly free of the tunnel—and Wonderman's influence—seemed dashed before it could really begin.

Suzie wondered if it would be the same for the others she'd met. She noticed Debbie and Steve engaged in conversation with an official-looking person. Steve appeared defensive, shaking his head firmly. She knew the way out would be even harder for them, if it was even possible at all.

"Where's Wonderman?" she asked Robbie.

"Swept away. They're looking for him now, but they doubt he survived. We were lucky to make it out ourselves."

"Where's…?" she began to say, and then it was Herb who whispered to her. It was her father who sighed Jazz's name.

"Jazz?" she said, staggering over to the second ambulance. There was a whirlwind of activity. A medic was attaching an IV, another pumping the chest of the man who lay there before her. Then, Suzie saw the blood. How could she not have realized?

"Jazz!" she shouted. She pushed someone out of the way, and got down by his side. His eyes fluttered, his stomach lying exposed, blood pooling on the ambulance floor. The paramedic gave up pumping.

"Wonderman's parting gift, knifing me right here in the stomach. But it's okay. I'm free. I'm going to see her again, I'll be with Judy again soon…"

Suzie was crying now.

"You can't die. You can't let that asshole win!" Suzie said, holding Jazz's hand. It was cold and limp. She could feel his strength ebbing away. "Don't die, Jazz. You can still get free. You can still have a life topside, up here out of the tunnel," Suzie sobbed.

Jazz smiled up at her.

"Suzie, I'm happy, believe me. It's my time to go. Just remember you got people who love you. It don't matter about anything except they love you. Just promise me this, get yourself a life away from here. D'you promise me?"

Suzie nodded as the tears flowed.

"Remember Judy, won't you? I'll be seeing her soon. We'll be back together soon…"

"Ma'am, you have to stand aside, now."

A paramedic was next to Jazz, and Suzie understood she had to step away, and yet her feet wouldn't move.

"Jazz, don't leave us… I can't say goodbye."

Jazz closed his eyes. He smiled faintly as his breathing grew increasingly labored, as his heart rate slowed precipitously, as he began to leave this world and all he knew in it.

Robbie held Suzie close.

"It's over," he said.

Epilogue

The first notes were struck. They hovered and swayed, just like the flecks of dust twinkling in the shaft of sunlight that beamed into the room. Suzie put down the tablet she was reading, about the floods and the moles who were still unaccounted for, Wonderman among them.

She looked over at the piano and nodded at the familiar man who'd sat down and begun to play Chopin's *Ballade Number 1*. As the notes washed over her, she laid there, listening intently, a smile playing on her lips.

This time, she knew it wasn't her father who performed, though this was his favorite piece of music—and hers too. This time, she knew she was experiencing the real world in this clean, welcoming place, where the sunlight danced, and the shadows had finally begun to recede. This time, she knew the man playing the piano was also a resident of this facility, the same one she'd been receiving treatment within.

The voices in her head had been slowly fading, as the medication began its work, stitching together the fragmented parts of her mind, settling down the chaos and disorder. The voices hadn't entirely disappeared—the doctors here said they may never stop completely, but she was content to live with them, now that they were more quiet, kinder?

If she glanced sideways, she could still see the two schoolgirls sticking their tongues out at her, but they didn't say anything anymore. She knew for sure now that they weren't real.

And the other voices, the older woman who told her to cut herself, and the stern man, had trailed off, like they were speaking to her from a place faraway. Perhaps they would leave her completely—or perhaps they'd stay. It was too soon to tell.

Her father's voice whispered to her now and then, but he too had drawn back into the recesses of her mind. She found —more and more—that she was living in the world outside of all that now.

When Dana told her she'd found a place for her in a residential facility, where there were people experienced in treating conditions like hers, she didn't fight this time. She only nodded, knowing she had to do this for her mom—the only real mother she'd ever known.

With her eyes shut, Suzie allowed the soothing piano notes to seep down deep into her soul. But then, she sensed someone sit down next to her. She didn't have to open her eyes to know who it was. She could feel his warmth, his steady presence, and she knew it was Robbie. She smiled as he took a gentle hold of her hand, as together, they listened to the music fill the tranquil space.

Perhaps soon, they would all go home.

Did you love *The Mole People*? Then you should read *Myface* by Kevin Landt!

Catfishing can be a deadly business, especially when social media mega-influencer Angela Fox has you in her sights.

Available on Barnes & Noble

www.ingramcontent.com/pod-product-compliance
Lightning Source LLC
Chambersburg PA
CBHW021448150726
47989CB00001B/441